THE PREACHER'S KID

THE PREACHER'S KID

A Novel

L.A. Holly

Writers Club Press
San Jose New York Lincoln Shanghai

The Preacher's Kid
A Novel

Writers Club Press
an imprint of iUniverse, Inc.

For information address:
iUniverse, Inc.
5220 S. 16th St., Suite 200
Lincoln, NE 68512
www.iuniverse.com

ISBN: 0-595-22491-1

Printed in the United States of America

For Dad,
Whose strength was my haven,
Whose love was my fortress,
Whose faith was my beacon,
And whose journey here was way too short.
I love you, Dad, and miss you every day.

And For Mom,
You have always been the one taking care of everybody, even when it should have been us taking care of you. Without your unconditional love, unquenchable spirit, and unconquerable faith this book would not exist, nor for that matter would its author. With every fiber of my being, I love you.

Contents

Prologue: Forty East. 1
Chapter 1 Wabash, The Naked Cannonball 3
Chapter 2 Just As I Was...Amen! 9
Chapter 3 Contents Under Pressure 21
Chapter 4 Grave Trouble 35
Chapter 5 Unconditional Love...And Other Strange Dreams 49
Chapter 6 Fighting Back 57
Chapter 7 Sudden Death 69
Chapter 8 This Was Heaven 83
Chapter 9 Forty West 95
Epilogue: Better Late Than Never 115
About the Author 117

Prologue: Forty East

July 17, 1991

When you're traveling east on Interstate Forty, somewhere between Albuquerque and Amarillo, and every mile you drive looks exactly like the one before, and the road is as straight as a sunbeam, and the cruise control is set at seventy, and you are not too punch drunk from the hypnotic effects of the warm sun and the stripes in the road zipping rhythmically by, you have time to think.

That is what I am thinking. That, and how much a life can change with just a phone call. I am thinking that this journey is not just a sixteen-hundred-mile trek back to the home of my boyhood. No. It is a journey back...in time.

Time. I am thinking about how swiftly it has flown and how far it has removed me from the simpler days of my youth. I am headed for a town of seven hundred souls, where I was mostly raised, when just last night I was selling a shiny new Jaguar, my favorite import, to a businessman in a tailor-made suit, in the carnival-like world that is downtown San Francisco.

❧ ❧ ❧

I am thirty years old now. Single…still. And trying my best to remember how in God's name I got from Rooster, Texas to San Francisco, California. Neither world could even imagine the existence of the other. And somehow, I have lived in both. Separately. But sometimes, it seems, simultaneously.

I turn it over again and again in my mind, trying to connect the two worlds, and reconnect, if possible, with the world I left and now return to. The sadness in my breast is so heavy, it feels like a tumor. My eyes are swollen from twelve hours of almost constant crying. I need a happy thought. I need a better place. I need a haven to run to, mentally.

❧ ❧ ❧

A jackrabbit stirs in the baking New Mexico sun and darts for the North side of the highway. He makes it to my right front tire and there his life ends. I feel the thump, thump. And I feel again the sadness, the heartache, the loss. And the tears come uninvited and uninhibited, burning in the tracks they make in my cheeks.

❧ ❧ ❧

Come on now, Reg. This is a long trip. Pace yourself. Pull yourself together!

I am thinking now about Rooster. About my parents and sister and friends. Things were not perfect. Once, they were even tragic. But life was good. It all made sense somehow. Not like now.

But that was then. I was a kid, hanging on every word my dad said. I was a boy full of life and life was full of wonder.

That was then…

CHAPTER 1

Wabash, The Naked Cannonball

I stood on the top step of the baptismal tank, wearing nothing but a smirk. I was there in answer to the double-dog dare of my uncle, Roy Henderson, who was three years my elder and who served alternately as my companion and my nemesis. This day, he happened to be both.

"You won't do it, chicken-liver," Uncle Roy—which he loved to call himself, just to keep me in my place—challenged again.

"Oh yeah, watch this!" I said defiantly, and then launched my skinny-as-a-rail, four-foot frame high into the air. I pulled my knees to my chest, locked my hands around them, closed my eyes and prepared for impact. It came with a vengeance. When my naked bottom slapped the ice-cold water, I gave out a yelp. I traveled through the water like a projectile, quickly reaching the even-colder stainless steel bottom with a thud. Gathering my feet beneath me, I paused ever so briefly, basking in the glory of my conquest, my mind on fast-forward, thinking of how my friends and my hero, Roy, would tell stories and maybe even sing songs about my daring deed.

Then, with all my might, I uncoiled, shooting to the surface with such force that I rose in all my glory three-quarters of the way out of the water, arms stretched above my head, fists clenched in victory. Settling into a dog paddle, I shook my head, rubbing the water from my eyes.

"See, I told you I would…"

Just then a very large, powerful hand like an iron clamp locked itself about the nape of my neck. I looked to the far side of the baptistery where Roy had been standing, but he wasn't there. In the instant I had jumped, he had bolted down the stairs and out the back door. *Vanished. The deserter!* And I was left alone to face the wrath of the menacing behemoth known as Deacon Broadas. (Which is pronounced BROADus, but we kids had our own, less flattering pronunciation of his surname.)

Joe Broadas was big, he was tough, and he was intolerant of deviant behavior of any kind, especially in the house of God! He was retired from the Marine Corps. I think he must have been a Drill Sergeant or some such. He was also a widower. (Roy told me that he had his wife executed for bad behavior—a downright lie which I fully believed until some years later when I mustered the nerve to quiz my mom about it.)

It seemed to my comrades and me that this pillar of the church was generally a miserable being whose primary function in life was to make everyone around him equally unhappy.

He was also my Sunday school teacher, and the church custodian.

"Reginald Reynolds!" Broadas boomed from beneath his thick mustache, dragging me to the steps where my unprecedented flight had begun. "What in the thunder do you think you're doing?" ("What in the thunder…" I never quite understood that phrase, although I heard it quite often. Mom said it was "Baptist cussing." Her theory was that since we Baptists frowned so on cussing, we made up substitutes. I guess she's right. There were other frequently used phrases like "Blue blazes," "Tarnation," "Dadgum," and my dad's favorite, "Cotton-pickin'.")

Of course, I did not have an answer for Deacon Broadas' query, so I said, "Nuttin."

"Dry yourself off, boy, and get dressed immediately," he commanded, handing me a wadded-up towel. "You and I are going next door."

Oh, no! Not that. Anything, please, anything but that. Perform Chinese water torture, if you must or just kill me like you did your wife, but don't take me next door. Thoughts like these collided inside my head with imagined attempts at escape. I could feign illness, maybe. Perhaps temporary insanity would fly. *No. Wait a minute. I lost something...a ring. It fell into the tank and I was trying to get it...*Or, I could run. Surely I could outrun the old, heavy-footed, thick-bodied deacon. Instead, I just shivered and muttered, "Yes sir."

Did you ever hear of the Trail of Tears? It seemed to this transgressor that the trip next door was just such a passage. That short journey down the stairs from the baptismal dressing room, out the side door of the sanctuary, down the darkened hallway leading to the back of the church, through the kitchen and out onto the back porch was like a Death March to me. I stood for a moment on the porch, waiting for the deacon to secure the door, and squinted against the bright sunlight, hoping against hope that my grandfather's car would be gone. It wasn't. His brand new maroon Ford LTD was parked right in front of the modest two-bedroom, white wood-frame parsonage, signaling like a beacon that Pastor Austin Wayne Henderson was home.

Big Granddad, as we grandkids called the Reverend A.W. Henderson, showed no emotion as Deacon Broadas presented an impassioned case for swift and certain justice. When the self-appointed eye-witness/prosecuting attorney finished, my grandfather thanked him politely, assuring him justice would be served and that his services, though greatly appreciated, were no longer needed.

For a long moment the deacon just stood there, rocking on the balls of his size thirteen black-booted feet, looking from Big Granddad to me and back again. It appeared he wanted to say more, but thought better of it. Finally, he wheeled about like the military man he was, and marched out. The screen door banged a few times behind him and then latched. It sounded oddly like the hammering of nails into a coffin. My coffin.

Wait a minute! Is that Taps I hear playing softly in the distance? Goodbye, cruel world.

Big Granddad's prowess as a disciplinarian was legendary. Mostly, it was Roy, the youngest of his six children, and his only son, who perpetuated the legend. He had filled my fertile mind with ample seed to produce a mighty crop of fear and loathing.

And, brother, it was harvest time in the Henderson house.

Really, Roy's own experience on the business end of Big Granddad's leather barber's strap (with which, I felt certain, he could fell a sizable tree) was rather limited. It wasn't that the mighty A.W. Henderson was reluctant to discipline his boy. No, it was just that Roy was so dadgum good at doing unchristian things without getting caught! Boy, did I admire him for that.

My own fortune in such matters, as in this instance, was something else entirely.

To this point I had never had occasion to be disciplined by Big Granddad. My parents took turns handling those duties. (I can't recall for sure, but I think it was Dad's turn.) But they were gone to Fort Worth for a couple of days, looking at used cars at the Tarrant County Auto Auction. Dad owned a small but prominent used car lot on Hubbard Street, the main drag through Mineral Wells, Texas, and once a month or so he would make the forty-mile pilgrimage east to Cowtown to buy cars. So, my younger sister, Rachel, and I found ourselves the unhappy wards of Big Granddad and Gramma.

* * *

Somehow I survived the whipping that came mightily upon my person that day. I know that more delicate souls prefer the word "spanking" to "whipping," but then they never got a whipping from Big Granddad. The licks he gave me raised whelps on my posterior and the backs of my thighs, the traces of which did not completely disappear for over two weeks. (The red stripes evenly dispensed across my linen white rump, accompanied as they were by deep blue bruises, would later prompt Roy to place his hand over his heart and pledge allegiance to the American flag.)

I must have cried for thirty minutes, until Big Granddad came back into Roy's bedroom, where I had been banished and threatened more of the same if I did not "dry it up." Forcing myself to stop bawling wasn't easy, and I got the hiccups trying. So, for the next half-hour I would rhythmically sniff, then hiccup. Sniff. Hiccup. Sniff. Hiccup.

My butt and legs were on fire, my ribs were sore from sniffing and hiccuping, and my pride was wounded because I couldn't quit crying. But, I lived to tell the story. And among my peers, all of them possessing a holy fear of the big Baptist preacher, that was considered no small feat. Besides, I had also bravely protected the anonymity of my accomplice, furthering my legend.

And so, on that warm summer day in nineteen sixty-eight another chapter was written into the lore of the Walters Baptist Church of Mineral Wells, Texas. I was known throughout the elementary department as "Wabash," in honor of my naked cannonball. It was a glorious title, and I wore it proudly.

I was six years old, *going on seven!*

CHAPTER 2

Just As I Was…Amen!

"Hell is a terrible place of fire and brimstone! It is the place where the worm dieth not and the fire is not quenched. It is a place created for the punishment of Satan and his army of imps, and reserved for all those who reject Jesus Christ as Savior and Lord of their lives."

Sammy Sneed was not an educated man. He never even graduated from high school. But, boy, could he sermonize! He was both eloquent and abrupt. When he spoke of the love of God one could almost hear the rustling of angels' wings. And when he described Hell and all its horrors it was hot enough to send sinners scurrying to the altar. This slight, little man, who was not more than sixty inches tall, and weighed in at no more than a buck twenty, stood at least ten feet tall when he preached. But it seemed to me that he never stood straight up. His whole body would tilt forward, like he was leaning into his sermon for emphasis. At first, I was sure he was going to lean too far and go crashing to the floor. I even punched my friend, Gib, and predicted it. But he never did. Instead, he simply worked his own brand of gospel magic, mesmerizing every soul in the congregation. All thirty-five or so of us.

"God doesn't want you to go to Hell. In fact, He loves you so much that He sent His Son, Jesus Christ, to Hell for you. That's right! When

Jesus died on that old cross he entered into the very pits of Hell and snatched the keys to death and the grave from the hand of Satan. And then on the third day He burst forth from that tomb—triumphant over death, sin and Hell. And now He offers His atonement to anyone who will call upon Him. I am asking you to make the decision of a lifetime. It is too important to ignore, too urgent to hesitate. Come! Trust Jesus and be saved."

With those words hanging heavily in the air and on the minds of us listeners, Brother Sneed brought his sermon mercifully to a close. I found myself standing between my mother and Gib, both hands locked in a death grip on the back of the pew in front of us, fighting back tears and the overwhelming urge to fly to the front and throw myself onto the little maple-colored, wooden altar. I was engulfed in a sense of utter despair. The lump in my throat made it almost impossible to swallow. With my eyes tightly shut at the preacher's command, I just knew he was looking straight at me. I could feel it. He had a piercing gaze that I was sure would make a grizzly shiver. Oh yes, I was certain of it. Though I dared not peek, I knew he was looking at me and through me, right down into my dirty, sinful heart.

Just as I am without one plea,
But that thy blood was shed for me
And that thou bidst me come to thee,
O Lamb of God, I come. I come.

My father led the congregation through that first verse of the Invitation hymn. No one went forward, so the evangelist instructed him to sing another, and then another. With each succeeding verse the knot in my stomach grew tighter. By the fourth—and if no one moved, we were assured it would be the last—verse, all power to resist was drained from my soul. I knew what I had to do. Casting aside my inhibitions, I stepped past my mother and into the center aisle. My father stopped the invitation mid-verse, threw down his songbook, and sprinted past the podium and evangelist, descending the two platform steps in a single bound. He met me in front of the altar (I'm not sure, but I think he jumped it to get to me), dropped to his knees, and gave me one of his patented bear hugs. "Son," he whispered into my ear, "why did you come forward tonight?"

❧ ❧ ❧

My Dad was a big man. At least he always seemed so to me, although I have come to realize now that I am grown that he was really just a medium-sized fellow who happened to be about sixty pounds overweight. He was six feet tall, with shoulders that were a bit narrow and hands and feet that were small and puffy. In fact, he was puffy all over, especially about the midsection. He had a jolly, round face accented by thick eyebrows and brownish-green eyes that danced when he laughed and seemed to smolder whenever he was beset by a foul temper. The hair around the circumference of his head was also thick, as were his Elvis-style sideburns. But he was as slick as a marble slab on top. The crown of his head always looked shiny, as if he kept a fresh coat of wax on it. He would joke that he operated a mosquito skating rink up there. Dad tanned easily, and during the summer months his face, forearms and the top of his head would bake to a deep, golden brown. That made him quite a sight when he was lounging about the house in his shorts and muscle shirt, because the rest of his body never caught a ray of sun, and remained milky white. He had the same markings as my Uncle Roy's collie, Troubadour!

Daniel Lyman Reynolds was lovable, too. Everybody thought so. He was the jolly fat guy, quick-witted, fun and full of life. He never smiled—he grinned. And when he grinned he used his whole face. Even the top of his golden-brown head would wrinkle up in laughter. He loved to tell jokes and he loved to sing. And he never forgot a punch line or a lyric.

Dad was highly intelligent, even though he only completed eleventh grade in school before quitting to go to work and help support his aging father and sickly mother. His brain could store and retrieve information with amazing accuracy. Consequently, he was a formidable foe and invaluable partner when the family got together for an evening of forty-two. (Forty-two is an immensely popular domino game of suits and trumps—and a Texas tradition.) In fact, he and Big Granddad had established themselves as legends in the game in the late fifties, teaming up to win three consecutive Texas State Forty-two Championships.

They retired from tournament play after their third title. Yep! They went out on top, a fact Roy and I were always fiercely proud of, and one that we used unmercifully in the my-dad's-better'n-your-dad arguments boys so often engage in. After all, not many dads in Palo Pinto County had been featured on the cover of *Texas* Magazine.

The inconsistency of meticulously teaching us to play forty-two, while strictly forbidding us to touch a deck of playing cards never occurred to Roy or me. At least, not until some years later.

My dad had three great loves in his life: his God, his family, and cars—usually in that order. His devotion to God and family was the result of his godly mother's influence on his life. She was a devout woman, I am told, whose whole world revolved around her only child to live beyond infancy. She lost the three before Dad, two girls and a boy, to crib death. At least, that's how the coroner's reports read. Who knows? So many things that are clear today in the field of medicine were mysteries then.

With such immeasurable suffering as would accompany the loss of not one, or two, but three children, one might have expected Alva Mae Reynolds to question or doubt her God. She never did, though. Not as far as anyone could tell.

I never knew my paternal grandmother. She died the very day I was born. While my mother was giving birth to me in the maternal ward on the third floor of Palo Pinto County General Hospital, my grandmother was in the basement in intensive care, sighing and moaning away her very life, fighting a losing battle with diabetes. Just three hours after welcoming his firstborn to the world, Dad watched his mother die.

Dad often recounted the story of my birth and his mother's death in his sermons, coupling the two together, as though they were a single event. It was an illustration that served him well. He would use it to point out the brevity, fragility or uncertainty of life. Or, he would use it to remind us that even our greatest sorrows are tempered with joy, or vice versa. Regardless of the context in which he told the story, he would always end it by saying, "The Lord giveth and the Lord taketh away; blessed be the name of the Lord."

Frankly, Dad's use of the story made me uncomfortable. Partly, because he would usually weep as he told it. Did he somehow blame me for my grandmother's death? Even if he didn't, I did. Some little irrational corner of my conscience bothered me.

It probably didn't help my psyche any that my birthdays, no matter how joyously celebrated, were always concluded by a family trip to the cemetery to place flowers on my grandmother's grave. Ecstasy mingled with bitter sorrow. Celebration and mourning. Such has been my life. Such was the life of my father.

Dad's love for cars explains his ownership of the little used car lot in Mineral Wells. Reynolds' True Value Motors, which is still in the family, owned and operated by my younger sister, Rachel, and her second husband, Bryce, now occupies a newer, more modern facility, and boasts a staff of five salesmen, an office manager, and a secretary. But in Dad's day, it was just he and my mom in a little two-room office building on the corner of Hubbard and Northeast Twenty-Fourth Streets. He did all the buying and selling and managing. She notarized transactions and kept the books. He loved the work and so did she. And they worked well together, seldom arguing. God as my witness, I can count on one hand the number of times I have seen my parents fight. He worshiped her; she catered to him. And they both loved cars.

Of course, they loved God, too.

It was their love for God and all things to do with the church that created the dichotomy that was our lives. Dad was BI-. No, not bisexual; bi-vocational. For years, he was what we call a lay preacher; one who felt called to preach, but continued to earn his living in the secular realm. He would fill in at the Walters Baptist Church whenever Big Granddad was out of town or ill. He also filled the pulpit for other little churches in surrounding communities, including the tiny Calvary Baptist Church in Rooster, Texas.

When the Rooster church lost their pastor to a larger congregation in Dallas, they wasted no time in calling Dad to come and fill in for them. A bond quickly developed between church and preacher, and less than one month after their former pastor of seventeen years had resigned, the church issued a unanimous call to my father to become their permanent pastor. He was only the third man to fill the position in the church's fifty-three year history.

Dad's new position was considered permanent, but could not be called full-time. The congregation consisted of only ten faithful families, a handful of occasional attendees, and a few who wandered in once or twice a year, just to check things out. They could not financially support our family of four. And that, I am convinced, was a relief to Dad, because it meant he would be obliged to continue operating the car lot. The fact that his new double life would require a daily thirty-five mile commute between Rooster and Mineral Wells did not phase him in the least, either. He said to me, "Son, there are few things in life better than the feel of the wheel in your hand, the wind in your hair, and the hum of a good motor."

Dad was a Cadillac man. Our family car was a chocolate brown Sedan Deville. But his toy, his pride and joy was his 1967 Cadillac El

Dorado, a sporty red convertible that seemed to catch everyone's eye, in Rooster and in Mineral Wells.

So, we sold our little, three-bedroom tract home in Mineral Wells and bought a landmark in Rooster. That's right. The big, two-story, turn-of-the-century house that stood awkwardly atop the biggest hill in town was a local landmark. We even had the bronze plaque beside the front door to prove it. I read the thing numerous times, but can't remember what it said, except that the house was built in eighteen sixty-nine. It was the oldest house in town. It was in pretty good repair, too. Built like so many Texas homes of that era, it had a huge front porch that ran across the entire front of the house.

A few paces to the right of the big mahogany front door Dad hung a wooden porch swing. He and Mom would sit there in the cool of the evening, her head on his shoulder, and they would dream and plan and love each other. Sometimes, they would call Rachel and me to join them. If I close my eyes, I can still feel myself in Dad's lap, his breath on my neck, the air pungent with the strange, sweet aroma produced by the ever-present blend of Right Guard deodorant and Aqua Velva after shave.

He would say, "Momma, have you ever seen two rottener kids?"

And she would say, "Never."

And we knew we were loved.

Though my experiences there were sprinkled with such precious moments, still I hated that old house. And, I felt sure it hated me, too. At night, when I was all alone in my upstairs bedroom, while Mom and Dad and Rachel slept downstairs, the house would creak and moan and whisper things inaudible and yet sinister into my ear. My pride, already over-developed, would not permit me to call out for Dad or request a transfer to the empty downstairs bedroom in the southeast corner of the house, just two doors down from my parents' room. Instead, I slept with my Jim Sundberg autographed baseball bat under the covers with me, prepared to spring into action and defend myself against whatever evils lurked in the dark shadows around me.

Mom had put me upstairs to give me privacy and a place to play with my friends that was out of the flow of traffic. She also thought I would enjoy the beautiful view of the town available through the bay window located directly above the front door and just beyond the foot of my bed.

She was right. It was a majestic view, especially at night when the twinkling lights of the little town were set against the backdrop of the rolling Texas hills. avI often climbed out onto the roof, laid on my back, hands locked behind my head, and stared up at the stars and dreamed big dreams and made big plans. It was also great when my friend, Gib, spent the night to have the whole upstairs—which consisted of my bedroom, a bedroom converted into a study, a bathroom, and an attic storage room—to ourselves. It made quite a fort! But all the sleepless nights I spent fearful in my bed, begging God to hasten the morning sunrise seemed an awful price to pay for those scant benefits.

Hillside Drive, the road linking us to civilization, started at our driveway and ran straight down the side of the steep hill northward and through the heart of town, dead ending into Main Street. At the foot of the hill, where Hillside Drive and Lovers' Lane intersected sat the Calvary Baptist Church. The church was situated on the north side of Lovers', so that our house and the church building faced each other.

Calvary Baptist Church was a narrow building, covered with red brick at the bottom and white asbestos siding above the brick. It had only two entrances: one in front and one in the back. Atop the steep roof sat a tall, stately steeple, crowned with a cross. The steeple was too large for the little church, and it seemed to me to unnecessarily raise the expectations of those who saw it from a distance. There were also six multi-colored stained glass windows, three on either side of the sanctuary, each depicting a scene from the life of Jesus. The windows were tall and arched and painted a kaleidoscope of colored patterns on the white walls and wooden floor of the sanctuary, the colors and patterns constantly changing as the sun worked its way across the Texas sky.

The sanctuary could accommodate maybe eighty worshipers. There were two rows of eight wooden pews each. The pews, like the altar and podium, were maple-colored. They were hard, too, and uncomfortable, making it nearly impossible for a ten year old boy to "sit still and be quiet," no matter how much his mother threatened.

But on that particular Friday night, when Sammy Sneed was preaching the final service of a five-day revival meeting, I had no trouble sitting still and listening to the white-haired preacher. There was something making me far more uncomfortable than a hard pew. I was plagued by the terror of an uncertain eternal destiny. I did not want to go to Hell. I wanted Jesus in my heart.

"Son, why did you come forward tonight?"

Why did I come forward? Isn't it obvious? Can't you see?

"I gotta get saved. I need to ask Jesus into my heart." I buried my face into my father's chest and cried. Yes, I cried. Like a baby. And for the briefest of seconds I thought, *I hope Gib can't see me crying.* But, as quickly as that thought came, it vanished. I really didn't care who saw. I didn't care who knew. I needed to get saved! And that was all that mattered right then.

I didn't realize that Mom had been right behind me as I went to the altar from our fourth-row pew. She was sitting on the front pew in her pretty pink dress, the one she covered with a pink and purple and white flowered polyester jacket. She was wiping her tears with a tissue she had taken from her purse. When Dad looked up at her, she nodded knowingly and handed him his big, black King James study bible. Dad took the Bible, turned toward the altar, pulling me to my knees beside him, laid his bible on the altar and began to thumb through the pages. His puffy hand trembled with excitement as he carefully maneuvered through the well-worn, slightly yellowed pages; sometimes pausing to gently pull two pages apart that had been stuck together.

I knew by heart the texts Dad would read to me. They were some of the first scriptures I had been taught and encouraged to memorize in Sunday School. The Drill Sergeant-turned-deacon, Brother Broadas was emphatic about bible memorization. He even rewarded it with hot fudge sundaes at Dairy Queen.

"Son," Dad began, "the Bible says in Romans 3:23, 'All have sinned and come short of the glory of God.' Do you understand what that means?"

"Yessir."

"What does it mean, Son?"

"It means that everybody is a sinner. We, um, we all do bad things."

"That's right." Dad's voice glowed with approval. "Now, look here in Romans 6:23. Read what it says to me."

"'For the wages of sin is death, but the gift of God is eternal life through Jesus Christ our Lord.'" I half-read, half-quoted the passage.

"What is God telling us here, Son?"

"If we sin we die?" I answered quizzically.

"Well, yeah, sort of. He is saying that because we are all sinners, we all face death. But he is also saying that Jesus Christ, God's Son, came to earth to give us eternal life."

"But, we still die, right?" I had always been a little confused on that point. After all, Dad himself talked about how his own mother had been such a great Christian woman. But, she had died.

"Sure, we all die *physically*," Dad saw where I was going. "But we don't have to die *spiritually*."

"I don't understand," I confessed.

"People who die without the Lord go to a place called Hell. It is a terrible place of punishment. But the worst thing about it is that God is not there. You see, son, death is really just separation. Physical death is separation of the soul from the body. Spiritual death is separation of the soul from God."

"Oh." I wasn't exactly sure what dad had just said, but I knew he was right. He was my dad. And, he was my preacher. So, he had to be right.

I was not even aware that Evangelist Sneed had taken over leading the invitation hymn, led the congregation through all four verses again, and then encouraged everyone to quietly be seated while we finished our business at the altar. Mrs. Wise, the old church pianist, who despite a badly bent back played quite elegantly, flipped a few pages over in the hymnal and began to play *Amazing Grace* softly and slowly on the vintage upright Baldwin. Every eye in the house was on me, some prayerfully, others impatiently awaiting the outcome. Had I known they were watching, I might have become frightened or nervous. But I was oblivious to every single thing in the world except for my Dad, his bible, and my strong determination to get saved.

A few passages later, Dad closed his old King James, his left hand still gripping my shoulder, and said, "Son, are you ready to ask Jesus to save you?"

"Yes, sir!" I had never been more ready for anything in my whole life.

"Okay, then, let's bow our heads, and you pray."

"Dear Lord Jesus," I began cautiously, not wanting to confuse the matter in any kind of way, "I know that I am a sinner. And I am sorry for my sins. Jesus, please forgive me of my sin and come into my heart. I want to be your child." And, for good measure, just so we were completely clear on this issue, I added, "I do not want to go to Hell! In Jesus' name. Amen."

Now, Dad was bawling. So was Mom. She had moved to the altar, kneeling on the other side of me. They both hugged me. And then

Dad prayed. Oh, I had heard him pray a hundred times before, and have heard a thousand more since. But never did he pray more beautifully than he did right then. He thanked God for giving him such a fine son and for loving me and making me a child of God. And then he prayed what would become a kind of anthem in our house. "Lord God, please use my boy. He is yours now. Use him in a mighty way to do your good will."

I wasn't sure what all that meant. But it sure sounded good to me. So, I said, "Amen."

CHAPTER 3

Contents Under Pressure

Gilbert "Gib" Gillespie was maybe the only ten-year-old boy in the world skinnier than I was. He was basically a skeleton, tightly wound with wiry muscles and wrapped in a thin layer of pale skin. His face and forearms were smothered in freckles. His hair was an orange Brillo pad, so tightly woven that his mother broke the teeth out of combs trying to groom him. Gib preferred to keep his curly locks closely cropped. "High and tight! Like a marine," he said.

The day I met Gib—my family's first Sunday at our new church in Rooster—he wore a worn out short-sleeved vertically-striped shirt, with faded blue jeans. The jeans had holes in both knees and were a good two inches too short. But his mom was determined to get two summers' wear out of them, "If it hair-lips every cow in Texas!"

"That boy is sprouting like a doggoned weed," she said. "I can't keep shelling out money for new clothes every other week! And what he don't outgrow, he tears up. He's like trying to keep a bobcat clothed." Her constant complaining was really more explanation than exasperation. She knew that her son more often than not resembled an unmade bed. But, darn it! He was hard on clothes.

Gib also wore white (at least that was rumored to be the original color) tube socks, crumpled down around his ankles, and black sneakers with white racing stripes. He loved those shoes. Said they were the fastest in the whole fifth grade.

* * *

"Name's Gib." His pale blue eyes shined as he flashed me a toothy grin and offered his right hand: "Looks like me and you gonna have to be friends."

"Alright," I said, shaking his hand.

Gib bit his bottom lip and clamped down on my hand with all his might. His fingers were long, and there was deceptive strength in his bony hand. He studied my face as he squeezed my hand, hoping to catch some glimmer of surprise or sign of discomfort. But I pretended not to notice that the introduction had so quickly devolved into a contest. I smiled as pleasantly as I could under the painful circumstances and wriggled free from his death grip.

"Me and you gotta be friends," my opponent repeated, "'cause there ain't nobody else our age in this whole damn church."

Gib liked to cuss and did so, cautiously. Every now and again he would slip within earshot of his parents or some snitch. Then, he would either have his pants set on fire by a switching from his father, who carved his switches from a large weeping willow tree in their backyard, or his mother would wash his mouth out with soap. Sometimes, he got both.

The handshake was a contest; the cuss word was a test. Gib loved to engage in the former and administer the latter. Somehow, even in these first brief moments of our acquaintance, I sensed the gamesmanship that was afoot. And though his well-placed expletive caught me off-guard, I was careful not to register shock or displeasure. But I couldn't help glancing quickly over each shoulder to see if anyone else had heard. No one had.

"Really?" I said, "You mean there aren't any other kids our age in the whole church?" Having never been a part of a congregation so small, I was unprepared to accept such absurdity as fact.

"Nope. Closest one is my kid brother over there." Gib pointed to the seven year old Jesse, his physical and temperamental opposite. Jesse was plump and soft, like an overripe grape. Like his father, Stu, he was olive-skinned, dark-haired, short, and quiet.

By contrast, Gib was just a younger, male version of his Irish mother, Maggie, who always talked in cliches and colloquialisms. Maggie had a funny accent. It was an odd but entertaining mixture of Irish brogue and Texas twang. She was tall and thin, with a fair complexion, a quick wit and a fierce temper that blew in like a west Texas thunderhead and disappeared just as quickly.

Jesse was standing in the lunch line with his mother. She was helping him put barbecue, beans, and potato salad—which he didn't want but had to eat anyway—on his plate. The Sunday morning worship service ended at about noon, and everyone was invited to convene at the American Legion hall—which the church often rented on special occasions—for a fellowship to welcome the new pastor and his family.

The hall was just a couple of blocks from the church. It was a long, rectangular building , a former army barracks that had been bought from Fort Walters in Mineral Wells, and placed on pier and beams in its new location. The exterior was in desperate need of a fresh coat of paint, but inside, it was surprisingly well kept and up-to-date. On one end was a kitchen with two oversized porcelain sinks built into the long cabinet that stretched the length of the wall. On the other end the lodge members had built a tongue-and-groove hardwood dance floor.

Near the kitchen some of the men of the church had set up three eight foot tables end-to-end for the ladies to use as a buffet line. Those tables were filled with barbecue, beans, potato salad, Cole slaw, cornbread, an array of cakes and pies, and iced tea. Nothing was professionally catered or store-bought, either. It was all homemade. And it was all delicious.

Gib and I went through the line together. Gib was an incredible eater. He filled his paper plate way beyond capacity. It sagged and swayed under the weight of its treasure, threatening to collapse and make a terrible mess. But he managed it skillfully, without losing so much as a bean. After Gib ate his fill of the barbecue and beans, he got another plate and overwhelmed it with enormous slices of pie and cake.

"That boy has a hollow leg," Gib's mother said. "He eats like a horse. I swear, he's gonna eat me outta house and home."

I instantly liked Gib. He was like a Coke bottle that had been shaken hard or left in a hot place too long, always bubbling with life and ready to erupt.

"A live wire," his mother said.

Contents under pressure. That was Gilbert Gillespie.

❧ ❧ ❧

Dad moved us to Rooster the first week in August, 1971. He wanted Rachel and me to be able to start the academic year off in our new school. I was going into the fifth grade, Rachel into third.

Small towns can be hard on newcomers. Especially new kids. More especially, preacher's kids.

There were twenty-four kids in Mrs. Konnerup's fifth grade class. Every one of them had lived in Rooster their whole lives. Everyone except me.

The first day of school, Mrs. Konnerup, my new teacher, went around the room, making us each tell our name and one thing we would like for the others to know about us. I was petrified, frozen with fright. It would be a cinch for the others. They had gone to kindergarten, first grade, second grade, and third grade together. But what would *I* say to a room full of presumably hostile strangers? They hadn't invited me to their town, their school, or their classroom. Maybe they didn't want me there at all. None of them except Gib had ever seen me before that morning. And I caught them staring at me, like I was a Martian with antennae growing out of my head. I had hoped to just blend in, not call attention to myself. Maybe no one would even notice me if I kept real quiet. But, Mrs. Konnerup blew my plan with her sadistic scheme.

"Gib, we'll let you begin," said the teacher.

There were four rows of six desks in the classroom. Gib was placed in the front desk of the row farthest from the door and against the outer wall. (I later learned that it was unwritten school policy that Gilbert Gillespie be placed at the front of whatever classroom he was in.)

"Name's Gib. Not Gilbert. Gib. Best get that. And what I want you to know is that I can whup every last one of ya." He grinned, his straight white teeth sparkling, then added, "An' if I can't whup ya, I can durn sure outrun ya." He wanted to say "damn," but resisted the temptation. No sense getting sent to the office on the very first day of school. There was plenty of time for that.

The classroom erupted with a mixture of cheers and jeers. One of the girls crossed her arms in a show of disgust, rolled her eyes and said, "How mature." A few of the boys made farting sounds with their mouths. And two or three smart alecks shouted, "Amen, Brother Gilbert!"

Pandemonium seemed certain to set in. But it didn't. Mrs. Konnerup quickly regained control.

Maintaining control was not difficult for this Nazi commander-looking teacher. She looked mean and tough, with her thick arms and legs, short neck and wide head. Her eyes were gunmetal gray, and cold, her lips thin and tightly drawn across an overstated mouth. She had a jaw like Rocky Marciano, small ears that curled on both ends, and charcoal hair with a two-inch, white skunk stripe that started in her bangs just above her right eye and ran all the way through her shoulder-length bob. She wore a navy blue dress, navy stockings and black shoes. She was menacing, imposing, frightening in her appearance. "Ugly as a mud hen," I once heard Mrs. Gillespie say.

Konnerup knew it, and she used it to her advantage.

But beneath that beastly veneer beat the heart of a true beauty. Despite her rough exterior and carefully cultivated reputation, she was really a soft touch, generous, warm-hearted and kind. She loved her kids. Considered us her family.

Konnerup never married. Both of her parents had been dead for more than a decade, and her only sibling, an older brother lived in upstate New York with his wife and three kids.

Order restored, Colonel Konnerup continued with the introductions. (As far as we knew, we were the first class to confer the lofty title of "colonel" upon Mrs. Konnerup. But the name stuck, and became semi-official. On her thirty-eighth birthday, which we celebrated that year, we even commissioned Linda Kay Parker's mother, who owned a T-shirt shop in nearby Ranger, to affix the title to the back of one of our high school's football jerseys. We had her iron a large red number 1 on the front and back of the black jersey, and then print, "The Kernel," in white letters across the back shoulders. The spelling gaffe was not caught until she opened her present before us in class. She pretended to be displeased with our grammatical shortcomings, but in fact she treasured the gift, and wore it almost exclusively whenever she attended a school ballgame.)

Girls occupied all the other seats in Gib's row, and the first two seats in the next. This was no accident. It was tactical maneuvering by the Kernel. She knew full well Gib's capacity for stirring his brothers-in-arms to mutinous behavior. He was a miniature Andrew Jackson. All that energy and leadership quality! If only it could be harnessed and pointed in the right direction…

Most adults agreed that Gilbert Gillespie would either be a great American or a notorious criminal, depending on who got hold of him first, Jesus or the devil.

Yes, Gib could stir the boys up. But girls were another matter. Torment them? You bet. Agitate them? Whenever possible. But lead them? Wouldn't stoop so low. What good were girls if you couldn't pull their pigtails and mock them when you made them cry? Surround him with girls and he became an island, alone and isolated.

❧ ❧ ❧

Now, my own opinion of the fairer sex was pretty much in line with the one espoused by my new pal, Gib. Girls were a pain. Most of them were snitches. And, they were conspirators, too. Couldn't be trusted. That was my opinion.

At least, that was my opinion until that fateful moment when for the first time I was blindsided by the irresistible charm of Lori Anne Golden.

Gib's fiery diatribe was followed by a litany of humdrum, nondescript, typical prepubescent female gibberish. Gib addressed the student body with charisma and flare. The girls that followed him looked only at the teacher, or down at their feet. One of them even had a couple of fingers in her mouth, garbling her pathetic attempt at communication so that Ms. Konnerup had to admonish her, "Now, sweetie, you will need to take your fingers out of your mouth and speak up, so everyone can hear."

The girls were sweet. And they were shy. And they had mousy little voices. And I didn't hear a word they said. I didn't even catch their names.

Girls! Who needs 'em?

Of course, there was another reason I was unable to concentrate on what my female classmates were saying. I could actually hear my heart pounding like a bongo drum inside my ears. *Ba-boom, ba-boom, ba-boom.* With each completed introduction, my time of reckoning drew nearer. I would soon be forced to face Konnerup's kangaroo court. I was thankful to be sitting in the back seat of the first row. Sure, it meant that Gib and I were in opposite corners of the room. But at the moment the importance of that misfortune paled in comparison to the relief I felt at being the last student to have to stand and speak. There was still time. Anything could happen. A fire drill. A tornado. Armageddon. Not likely, but possible.

The last girl in Gib's row finished her mumbling and sat down. My heart rate quickened. *One row down, three to go.*

But then, there she stood beside her desk, the first desk in the third row, right next to Gib. That's when everything changed: my opinion of girls; my preoccupation with impending public humiliation; my heart's reason for running like a racehorse. I was suddenly and without warning taken captive by the most exquisite creature I had ever seen in all my ten years. Lori Anne Golden.

Her auburn hair was soft and shined with the glow of good health, bouncing playfully on her shoulders. When she spoke, my eyes were helplessly drawn to her heart-shaped lips. They were full and pink and always slightly puckered. The braces she wore on her teeth glistened when she talked and added a unique charm to her speech pattern. I especially liked to hear her say the letter 's.'

Lori Anne Golden did not put her fingers in her mouth when she talked. Nor did she stare at the teacher, or the floor. She didn't shuffle her feet or sway from side to side in embarrassment. She displayed none of the quirky habits I had come to expect from girls forced to speak to a crowd. Instead, she confidently faced her classmates, her iridescent green eyes sweeping across her audience, the nostrils of her small but perfectly symmetrical nose slightly flared.

"My name is Lori. Lori Anne Golden," she said and then fixed her gaze upon me. She looked into my eyes for a long moment, and I must have resembled a jackrabbit under a hunter's spotlight. I swooned. She continued, "I plan to be a lawyer when I grow up."

Then she whirled about, pointed her long, elegant finger at Gib and said, "You will probably be my first client, Gilbert."

"Haw, Haw! Very funny," said Gib, squirming uncomfortably under the commanding gaze of the most beautiful girl in the fifth grade.

Gib was temporarily tongue-tied, a rare sight, indeed. But not the rest of us. We roared with laughter. My classmates and I laughed aloud, together. It was the first time I had broken my silence since arriving on the school campus over an hour before.

The ice was officially broken, thanks to Lori Anne Golden.

I stole one more look before she sat down. I noted that she was about an inch shorter than me, which meant she was taller than every other boy in the class except for Gib and Chuck Illich, a freak of nature and future NBA forward. Lori was slender and graceful and sported a Coppertone tan, the result of a summer spent in her family's backyard swimming pool. She wore a green and blue plaid jumper over a white, short-sleeved Peter Pan collared blouse. Her clothes were crisp and new, and yet she wore them with ease. She was comfortable. I wasn't.

Neither was Gib. His cheeks were splotchy patches of red and white, and his ears looked like the taillights on a fifty-seven Chevy.

"Well said, my dear. Very good," said Ms. Konnerup, clapping her hands together. Then, she said to Gib, "You asked for that one, Gilbert," and winked. Gib's cheeks were now purple and red and white. But he was still sporting that big toothy grin. Sure, he was a little embarrassed, but he loved the attention.

After Lori, I didn't hear another word. Phil Farmer, a fat kid we called "Philsbury," because he looked so much like the Pillsbury doughboy, said something that made the whole class roar with laughter. But, I missed it. Nor did I hear Patrick Jones, or Willy Hernandez, or Monica Mallory, or any of the others.

"Ok, Mr. Reynolds. Would you like to introduce yourself to your new classmates?"

Reynolds. That name seems oddly familiar. Who do I know by that name?

"Are you ready, Reginald?" Mrs. Konnerup attempted to snap me out of my dazed stupor.

Ba-boom. Ba-boom. Ba-boom. The pounding in my ears was deafening. *Did she say my name?* I swallowed hard and blinked my eyes. Yes, she was definitely looking at me. I suddenly felt sick to my stomach. Standing on shaky legs, I braced myself against my desk, and licked my dry, cracked lips.

"My name is Reginal…uh, I mean Reggie, or…or just Reg."

Come on now, Reg! You can do this. Get hold of yourself. Easy, now.

I wanted so badly to make a good first impression. I wanted to be liked, to be accepted. I closed my eyes, licking my lips again, and struggled to gather my nerves.

And just like that, it happened. My mind that had been so confused, so cluttered, suddenly cleared, like the sun bursting through a great dark cloud. I felt an eerie calm, a clarity that would come to my rescue again and again throughout my life in similar circumstances.

"My family has just moved here. My dad is the new pastor of the Calvary Baptist Church. And," I paused here for emphasis, folded my arms across my chest like Superman, "now that I'm here, my new pal, Gib, is only the *second* fastest boy in the fifth grade."

"Hoo-wee!" shouted Phil Farmer, "Looks like the race is on, boys!"

Gib jumped up in his chair, "It's you and me, Preacher Boy!" Then he raised one foot so we could see his black sneaker with the white racing stripes. "Hope you brought your running shoes."

Mayhem ensued—short-lived. Order restored, Konnerup style.

⁂

When the first bell rang, signaling morning recess, every door in the Rooster elementary school building burst open, and kids streamed onto the schoolyard like ants to a Sunday picnic.

The Rooster Independent School District was so tiny that kindergarten through twelfth grade was all on one campus. The high school was a three-story red brick building that stood squarely in the middle of school property. On either side of the high school building, looking like flimsy glider wings attached to a jumbo jet body, was identical single-story, narrow buildings, each housing twelve classrooms, a restroom each for boys and girls, and nothing else. One wing served as the junior high, the other as the elementary.

It was the right wing from which one hundred, seventy-odd grade-schoolers scrambled. Most of the girls and the younger boys headed for the playground equipment, swarming the recently painted red and black merry-go-round, monkey bars and swings. A few of the girls just went to the park benches and picnic tables under the shade of a grand old oak tree to sit and talk and giggle. The older boys broke off into groups. Some headed for the baseball field to play kickball. Others had footballs and engaged in the schoolyard favorite, "Kill the man with the ball," or, "Smear the Queer" as Gib called it.

Only Konnerup's fifth grade class refrained from such revelry. Instead, we marched like toy soldiers towards the far end of the large freshly cut lawn, where the title of "fastest man in fifth grade" would be decided. Gib and I both sat down to re-tie our shoes while Philip Farmer removed his orange-brown Tony Lama cowboy boots, and used them to mark an imaginary starting line. Fifty yards or so down the field two girls stretched out a jump rope to mark the finish line.

Gib was cool and confident as he re-laced his undefeated racing shoes. His reign as fastest man in his grade had been challenged almost weekly since kindergarten, but he had never been beaten. For four years he had remained an undefeated, undisputed champion sprinter. He had no doubt in his mind that he would dispose of his braggadocios new pal with little trouble.

"Try not to embarrass me, preacher boy," Gib said. "We're pals an' I don't wanna have to make excuses for ya."

"I'll try."

I wasn't as cocky as Gib. But I wasn't really worried, either. Even as he rehearsed his pedigree and recited his multitudinous victories, I remained unimpressed. After all, at Travis Elementary in Mineral Wells, a much larger school boasting seven third grade classes, I had won runner-up in the fifty-yard dash on Field Day. As Gib executed his feeble plan to unnerve me, my mind wandered to the red second place ribbon I had draped over my little league all-star trophy on my dresser at home.

Besides, Travis elementary was about forty-five percent black kids. By 1971, most folks generally accepted their physical superiority in tests of speed. I had been the only white kid to even finish in the top ten! And in Rooster there was not so much as one black family, an oddity I didn't understand at all.

I figured I had been tested on a superior plane. Therefore, I tied my shoes confidently, sprang to my feet and did a couple of deep knee bends. "Hope you're ready to retire them things," I said, pointing to his beloved sneakers.

"Why?" Gib shot me a go-to-thunder look.

"'Cause I know it's gonna break your heart when you lose in them."

"Oh boy, now you're gonna be sorry, preacher boy. I ain't gonna let up on ya!" Gib still sounded cocky, but his eyes told another story. I saw a shadow of a doubt. My confidence was unexpected. That coupled with the fact that he had never seen me run made him just a little nervous.

"You girls wanna race, or what?" said Wee Willy Hernandez, the shortest kid in fifth grade, and the only Hispanic in the class. He was the self-appointed starter.

"Whaddaya mean girls? You're the one sings soprano, ya damn chili bean!" Gib loved to call Wee Willy various Mexican dishes. He also frequently mocked Willy's propensity for mixing up his 'sh' and 'ch' sounds when he talked. Gib would say something like, "Hey, Wee Wee, there's a shicken takin' a chit in your shair." And everyone would laugh, including the good-natured, unflappable Willy Hernandez.

"Ready!" shouted Willy. Gib and I toed the line with our right foot and crouched into running position. We both wore a cotton T-shirt, knee-length blue jean shorts, tube socks pulled past mid-calf, and sneakers. There was no distinct equipment advantage, unless you counted Gib's wonder shoes, which he had nicknamed "Black Magic."

"On your mark. Get set. Go!"

And we were off! I stumbled ever so slightly out of the gate, and Gib burst into an early half-step lead. Quickly steadying myself I tore down the field in typical sprinter style, my body tilted forward, head down, fists and feet pumping in rhythm like the pistons in dad's El Dorado. I loved to run. It felt so natural and effortless, like I was a low flying missile. I often imagined that I was Wile E. Coyote, with a rocket strapped to my back, sailing across the prairie, never touching the ground.

Gib, on the other hand, was more like Bugs Bunny: all knees and elbows. He ran straight up, swinging his arms in a wide arc, and alternately kneeing himself in the chest and kicking himself in the butt. He was gangly and awkward. But what he lacked in style, he more than made up in desire and effort. He could fly...like an albatross.

Gib clung tenaciously to his half-step lead for thirty yards. But my more fluid, aerodynamic style propelled me until at forty yards I had pulled even. Gib, stunned to see me in his peripheral vision, stole a glance in my direction, just in time to see me blow by him and finish a good two yards ahead. By turning his head, he threw off his rhythm, and as he crossed the finish line he stumbled, arms flailing wildly, long legs trying desperately to run under his toppling torso. The albatross was coming in for a landing, and as he did he fell head over heels, kneeing himself in the lip, and finally tumbling to a stop ten yards beyond the finish line.

The dethroned champion lay spread-eagle on his back, his bottom lip glistening with a trickle of blood, and the jump rope finish line entwined about his body.

But I had crossed the finish line first and glided to a graceful stop, my classmates cheering and whistling and hoisting me to their shoulders, like I had just finished a no-hitter in the seventh game of the World Series. "New world champion! New world champion!" they chanted as they carried me in a circle around my fallen opponent.

Gib sat up, chest heaving, and wiped the blood from his lip with his shirt. His pride was wounded, but his indomitable spirit was unbroken.

"Best two out of three!" He yelled.

But, I was saved by the bell, signaling the end of recess.

* * *

Fistfights and footraces. That about sums up my fifth grade year. Gib was the dominant influence in my school life, and when he wasn't challenging me to another footrace and losing, he was picking a fight with some other boy in the class, and winning.

Gib had some sort of code that precluded him from challenging me to a fistfight. I knew he was not afraid of me: I was more of a lover than a fighter. I didn't like to hit or be hit, unless it was on the football field. No, the fact was we were pals. I was his best friend, and that meant we didn't fight each other.

CHAPTER 4

Grave Trouble

Midway through that school year, Evangelist Sammy Sneed stormed into my life and I was converted on that frosty Friday night in December. The following Sunday morning I entered the chilly waters of a baptismal tank for the second time in my life. This time I was fully clothed, except for bare feet, and this time Deacon Broadas was nowhere to be found.

Dad stood in the middle of the baptistery and faced the congregation, a pair of brown rubber waders pulled to his chest, the sleeves of his white dress shirt rolled up past his elbows. I stood in front of him, the left side of my body to the audience. Dad had his left hand on my shoulder and his right hand, gripping a clean, white handkerchief, raised in the air.

"Son," Dad asked in a raised voice so all could hear, "have you accepted Jesus Christ as your Savior?"

"Yessir."

"Then, upon your profession of faith in Him, and upon the authority vested in me as a minister of the gospel, I now baptize you, my little brother in Christ, and son in the flesh, in the name of the Father, and the Son, and the Holy Ghost."

Bracing me between my shoulders with his left hand, and covering my nose and mouth with the hanky in his right, dad tipped me backwards into the water, until I was completely submersed. From my watery grave his voice was garbled, but I knew what he was saying. I had heard it many times before. "Buried in the likeness of his death." Then, lifting me up, he continued, "Raised in the likeness of his resurrection, to walk in newness of life."

The crowd erupted with a single voice in a loud "Amen!"

I shivered, my teeth chattering in the cold water, and wondered just how much my life would change. Would I be different? Dad said that when a person accepted Christ as Lord and Savior, "Old things were passed away, and all things became new."

❧ ❧ ❧

"What's it like?" Gib asked.

He and I were sitting on the rock fence that surrounded the ancient Rooster graveyard, one of our favorite hangouts.

We both loved to wander through the cemetery and read the inscriptions on the tombstones. Some of them dated back to the early eighteen hundreds. The most unique grave marker belonged to Robert Orrin James, the town's first sheriff, and founder of the First Baptist Church, who was said to be a cousin of the famous Jesse and Frank James. His tombstone, which stood eight feet tall, featured a three-foot bronze sculpture of Jesus in a pair of cowboy boots on top of a large white marble base. In the base was etched the inscription: "Robert Orrin James: Famous Lawman, Faithful Husband, Fearless Preacher of the Gospel. Born: January 31, 1803. Died: November 5, 1888."

"What's what like?"

"You know, being baptized. Man, you looked like a drowned chicken. You were shivering and your teeth were chattering. Were ya scared?"

"Naw!" I said, annoyed by the suggestion. "I was just cold, that's all."

"Yeah, but being dunked in front of all those people...I dunno."

I could see that Gib was in a rare, thoughtful mood. His normal playfulness and energy were held in check by his curiosity concerning conversion and baptism.

Then, it hit me. I was now a born-again Christian, and Gib wasn't. He was in danger of Hellfire, just like I had been. I suddenly felt anxious. I was just baptized six days ago on Sunday, and now here we sat, hunched down, coats drawn over our ears, backs braced against the cemetery fence, blowing into our hands to keep them warm, and I was going to Heaven and Gib wasn't.

My teeth began to chatter again. *Where's Dad when I need him? Gib needs to be saved. What am I going to do?* I felt an urgency, a need to help my best friend get things settled right there, right then.

"G—Gib."

"Yeah?"

"Have you ever, you know, asked Jesus into your heart?"

"Naw. I thought about it though. That same night you did, when that feller was here preaching, you know, the leaner? I almost went forward then."

"Why didn't you?" I asked. How much easier it would have been for me that night if my best friend would have gone with me.

"I dunno. Just didn't."

"You want to?"

"I s'pose. But, not right yet. I guess I'll wait." Gib was growing increasingly uncomfortable with the direction of the conversation he had started. So was I, for that matter.

"Hey," Gib said, a sudden resurgence of energy in his voice. "Wanna do somethin' fun?" Just like that he changed the subject, and I was relieved, and I was annoyed with myself for being relieved. Didn't I care that my best friend was going to Hell?

"Man, it's so cold," I said, teeth still chattering. The sky was gray and sunless, and a brisk north wind nibbled like a rat at my ears and fingers. "Let's just g-g-go to my house."

"Alright. But, first let's have some fun. Let's play football."

"You're crazy!" I protested. "There's nobody else to play with. Besides, we don't have a ball."

"Don't need a ball. Don't need nobody else, neither."

I was confused, but Gib quickly explained that he and I would be the team with the ball and all those dead people in the graveyard would be the other team. The goal was to run straight through the cemetery to the fence on the other side, which was the goal line. Any tombstones trying to tackle us, we would just knock down!

"We're the Cowboys; they're the Redskins. Let's go get 'em." Gib leaped to his feet, hollered, "Hut! Hut!" And ran to the tombstone nearest us. He hit it full-stride and the heavy marble rectangle toppled easily. Exhilarated by his initial victory, Gib waved to me, "C'mon, Preacher Boy! Hit somebody."

I did. I ran up to a tall, cylindrical marker and threw my weight into it. Down it went, thudding into the frozen, brittle ground. *That was easy!* Off I went to the next, and the next. Side by side, we cut a swath through the heart of the old burial grounds. Tombstones, some tall and stately, others short and dull, fell, defenseless before the charge of the mighty Dallas Cowboys!

As we neared the goal line, I came face to face with the marker of Roy Orrin James. I stopped. For an instant I thought I would leave the hallowed marker standing. But I was a shark, this was a feeding frenzy, and Roy James was raw meat. I lowered my shoulder and prepared to charge.

Whap! Someone hit me from my left side, sending me sprawling headfirst into the cold, hard earth. Dazed, I struggled to my feet, sure we had been caught in our sin, but it was Gib's voice I heard. It was he who had hit me.

"No, Preach," Gib said, shortening the nickname he had given me while trying to catch his breath, "Not the sheriff. He's on our side. He's a Cowboy."

The wind knocked out of me, I didn't try to argue or answer. Instead, I just nodded my head, and walked to the rock fence, leaning on it with my elbows, exhausted and disgusted.

Only moments before I had been intent on leading my friend to Christ. Instead, I had allowed him to lead me into sin. What kind of a Christian was I?

I didn't share my guilt with Gib. Instead, I listened to him blabber excitedly about how much fun that was, and pretended to agree. But he soon lost his enthusiasm, as the reality of what we had done sank in.

I pulled the hood of my coat over my ears and shoved my aching hands deep into the lined pockets. We walked up the hill to my house in silence.

Our turn-of-the-century house could be seen from nearly every point in the tiny town of Rooster. And, since our family loved Christmas so much, Mom and Dad felt it was incumbent upon them to properly decorate for the holiday, so everyone could share our joy.

As Gib and I trudged the long hill home, The sights and smells of the most wonderful time of the year invaded my senses. The roofline of the big house pulsated with the large red and blue and green bulbs Dad and I had strung only a week before. The big picture window between the front door and Dad's porch swing was also outlined with the bulbs, as was the bay window over the front door, and just beyond the foot of my bed.

Standing just inside the picture window, where the curtains were drawn so all could see, was the Reynolds family masterpiece. We had gone into the woods and found a Fir tree that was tall and full. Our house had ten-foot ceilings and Dad still had to trim nearly a foot off the top of our tree, just so it would fit. Mom and Rachel and I had begun stringing popcorn together the day after Thanksgiving. By the time we finished and mom dressed our tree with it, the string was so long that she had to wrap it around the tree twenty times to get it to fit. She also wrapped the tree in our gumball string and in multi-colored blinking lights. The branches were adorned with silver bells, gold and silver balls, and candy canes—my favorite decoration, because they became part of the spoils on Christmas morn.

A thin wisp of white smoke escaped from our chimney and hung suspended in the cold, damp air.

I have always loved the smell of a burning fireplace, especially in this part of Texas, where most people are burning cured mesquite and various forms of oak, creating an aromatic delight. It seems to signal that regardless of how harsh and brutal the winter and the world outside may be, there is always a place where warmth and love and security can be found.

In our front yard stood a majestic old Pecan tree, like a sentinel keeping watch over us and the fair citizens of Rooster. Besides the mighty oak in the Rooster schoolyard, our pecan was the most awe-inspiring tree in the whole town, some said in the whole county. Gib and I spent many a happy hour chasing each other through its branches, climbing up and up as high as we could go, until we would reach the thin branches at the top of the old tree, them bending and swaying beneath our weight.

Dad had sent me skinnying up the tree with a long string of the colorful blinking lights, just like the ones on the branches of our family Christmas tree. I went as high as I could go, and then I wound my way down, stringing the lights as I descended.

As Gib and I walked into the yard, he said, "Wow! Your dad do that?" He pointed at the blinking lights.

"Nope. I did." I was right proud of my work, too.

"Cool," he said, and then fell silent again.

Gib followed me onto the big front porch and through the mahogany door, where the assault on my senses intensified to such epic proportions that all thought of tombstones, phantom football, and evangelization dissipated. The graveyard was a bad dream. I had awakened, and only a foggy memory remained.

"Hi, boys!" Mom greeted us cheerfully. She was wearing one of her comfortable slipover housedresses and fuzzy pink slippers, her hair up in rollers and wound in toilet paper, as it was each and every Saturday night. She removed her favorite, overused, in-desperate-need-of-retirement potholder from her left hand and announced, "I just took a fresh batch of chocolate chip cookies out of the oven. As soon as they cool off a bit, I'll give you each a couple."

"That'd be great!" Gib answered enthusiastically. Obviously, he had pushed the graveyard incident out of his mind, too.

"Yeah, really great," I wholeheartedly agreed.

"Good! How about some hot cider, too?"

"You bet!" said Gib.

"Oh, yeah," said I.

In the fireplace a rip-roaring fire crackled and popped, the flames all red and orange and white and blue, dancing and leaping upon the firewood, casting a spell of serenity and nostalgia upon anyone who looked and lingered.

On the tree, the tiny lights blinked and twinkled, bringing the bells and balls and candy canes to life. Beneath her branches the Christmas bounty,—some wrapped in green and white and red Santas, others in silver and gold angels—had grown and grown, spilling out on every side.

On the wall opposite the fireplace, Dad's Sears and Roebuck console stereo was alive with the smooth, mellow voice of the King, Elvis Presley.

Mom loved Elvis. Really, she did. He was undoubtedly the only man alive with whom Dad would have been hard put to contend for her affection. That is, if Elvis had known Mom existed, or cared. She never got her pink Cadillac like Elvis drove, but Dad did see to it that she owned every album the king of rock and roll released, including the one now filling our living room with Christmas cheer.

Elvis' Christmas album was Mom's prize possession, or so it seemed. And she had been none too happy the Christmas before when her nine-year-old son scratched it trying to set the needle to replay his favorite song. To borrow from Mrs. Gillespie, "She was madder'n an old wet hen!"

So, as Gib and I waited anxiously for our refreshments, Elvis sang, *"I'm dr-dreaming of a white Christmas, just like the whu-one I used to know…"*

"Hey," said my observant friend, "That thing is skippin'!"

"Shhhh!" I said, finger over my mouth, then whisperng, "Don't remind her."

"Remind me of what?" Mom was in the living room now, bringing us our cookies and cider on her silver Christmas tray. "You mean, remind me of why Elvis stutters when he sings *White Christmas*?"

Oh, she's smiling. Good. I grinned guiltily, shrugging and accepting the goodies she had made me—and her forgiveness—with equal gratitude.

It's amazing just how long-gone any thought of tombstone football was from my mind when Mom announced that supper was served and Gib, who was now going to stay the night with me, and I sat down with my family to eat.

Dad, who got home late from Mineral Wells with the good news that he had sold three cars, was saying grace when there came a loud rapping at the front door. He finished praying, said, "Y'all go ahead and start. I'll be right back," and went to answer the door. I paid him no attention at all, filling my plate with chicken-fried steak, mashed potatoes, cream gravy, and fried okra. Gib worked with equal fervor, piling his plate high, scooping a huge bite of potatoes into his mouth, and saying between bites, “Mmm, mmm, Mrs. Reynolds, this sure is scrumptious.”

“Why, thank you, Gib,” she answered graciously. Then, “I wonder what is keeping your father, Reg. I’ll be right back.”

Dad had moved out onto the front porch and was in earnest conversation with our mysterious guest. Mom opened the door and then exclaimed in obvious surprise, “Oh! Deputy Conrad. How are you? Is everything alright?”

I choked on a big bite of steak, and had to cough it up.

Gib dropped his glass of iced tea on the floor.

We had both heard Mom greet Joe Conrad, a Palo Pinto County sheriff’s deputy, the one who lived in Rooster, and generally handled all the minor disturbances about town. I jumped from my chair, waving at Rachel, “Hurry! Go to the kitchen and fetch a towel.”

Gib and I were picking up the stray ice cubes and returning them to his uninjured glass. “Did you hear that?” I whispered.

“Yeah.”

“What are we gonna do?”

“I dunno. Maybe nuttin’. We don’t know why he’s here.”

“What if he knows?”

“I doubt it.” Gib was trying unsuccessfully to sound confident. “Even if he does, he don’t know it was us who done it. Nobody knows but you an’ me, and we have to keep it that way.”

Rachel handed me the towel and I wiped the tea off the hardwood dining room floor. *Boy, we’ve done it now. We are going to be in so much trouble. Someone prob’ly saw us.*

❦ ❦ ❦

“C’mere, boys.” It was Dad calling us from the living room. I quickly tried to determine if it was an angry voice, but I couldn’t tell. Gib and I came through the swinging wooden door separating the living and dining rooms to find Mom and Dad and Deputy Conrad standing in the middle of the room in a semicircle, with the deputy in the middle.

"Son," Dad addressed me, "Deputy Conrad here says there's been some vandalism at the cemetery. He wants to ask you and Gib some questions, alright?"

Vandalism. Did I know that word? It sounded so wicked, so criminal, so punishable-by-death.

"Ok," I said, "I guess so, but we don't know anything about it. Do we, Gib?"

"Shoot, no! I guess not." Gib looked really nervous, and guilty, and I have no doubt that I did, too. But Deputy Joe Conrad looked just as nervous. He was that way, though. Skittish, like a cat. He stood holding his white beaver skin cowboy hat, like all the county deputies wore, by the brim with both hands, shifting his weight from one black cowboy boot to the other, then back again. Even in my present state of terror, I thought he reminded me of Barney Fife from the Andy Griffith Show, and wondered briefly if Gib would agree.

The deputy cleared his throat and began, "Boys, there's been an incident of vandalism at the graveya…that is, cemetery, like Reverend Reynolds says."

Yeah, yeah. We know already. What's that got to do with us?

"It seems that fifteen tombstones have been pushed over."

Wow! Fifteen? Are you sure?

"We don't know yet who the perpetrators are."

Purple what?

I must have looked confused, because the deputy quickly explained, "A perpetrator of a crime is the person who did it. Like I said, we don't yet know who that is."

That's the best news I've heard all day! You are not going to find out, either. Not from us.

"Ol' Rufe Jones says he saw the two of you climbing the fence to the graveyard, or cemetery, earlier today. Now, understand this doesn't mean that we consider you suspects in this crime, we just thought you might be able to tell us if you know who did it, or if you saw anyone or anything that looked suspicious."

Gib spoke up first: "Well, we were there, alright, just hangin' out, ya know. But we don't know nothin' 'bout no tombstones bein' tumped over."

"How about you, Reggie," the deputy asked, "Did you see or hear anything unusual?"

Before I could answer, Gib blurted, "Oh, he couldn't of. He was with me the whole time. Ain't that right, Reg?" The fact that my pal suspended any use of a nickname in addressing me was an indication of the gravity of the situation.

"Well, no. I mean, yes. Gib's right. We were just there hanging out, leaning against the fence to get out of the wind. I didn't notice anybody else there."

"How long were you boys there?" The deputy was settling in to a less nervous, more professional tone.

"'Bout a half-hour, I'd say," answered Gib, our self-appointed spokesman.

"Mrs. Reynolds says you arrived here about 5:30, did you come straight home from the cemetery?"

"Yessir!" I snapped out the answer too quickly for Gib, so he just nodded his head in agreement.

"And, did you walk through the cemetery?"

A long, quiet pause. I shot a glance at Gib, and he at me. Not sure how to answer the question, Gib stumbled through his answer, "Well, yeah…but we never went through the part where the tombstones were pushed over. We, uh, we walked around the outside, alongside the fence. Huh, Gib?"

Instantly, the expression changed on every adult face in the room. The deputy's eyes got as big around as the cookies Mom had made earlier. His mouth dropped opened and he looked more nervous than ever. Mom took a full step back and covered her mouth with her hand, stifling a gasp. And Dad had a look on his face like someone had just swiped his shiny, red El Dorado. His green eyes went black, like two perfectly round pieces of coal. And his jaw muscle began to twitch the way it always did when he was angry.

I looked at Gib, and he at me. We both knew something had just gone wrong, but neither of us was sure what. The jig appeared to be up, and we were clueless as to why.

Again, the deputy cleared his throat, then he stammered, "Young man, what do you mean you never went through the part where the tombstones were pushed over?"

"Well, you know, out there in the middle of the graveyard where, where you told us they were tumped over."

"But, I never said those were the ones pushed over." *The heck you say! Of course you did, didn't you?* "Boys, you are hiding something and I think it is high time you come clean. This is a very serious matter. The best thing you can do is tell the truth."

That's when my smoldering Dad, who could remain silent no longer, jumped in, singling me out, "Reggie, you boys are lying, and I will not stand for it, you understand? Whatever you know, you better tell me. And I mean right now."

Dad's words were as fraught with dismay as they were filled with determination, and they landed on my conscience like an anvil dropped from the sky. My throat constricted with fear and dread and my Adam's apple felt like a softball lodged in there.

This was a side of his pastor Gib had never seen. What little color there was in my friend's features had all drained out. He looked like one of the white marble tombstones he had conquered scant hours before.

Gib was speechless. I wasn't. I opened my mouth, and spilled my guts.

❧ ❧ ❧

Silver bells, silver bells, It's Christmas time in the city.
Sleigh bells ring, ding-a-ling,

Soon, it will be Christmas day.

Oblivious to the fact that my orderly world was crashing down around me, Elvis continued to croon about the wondrous joys of Christmas, as if it wouldn't be cancelled, as if anyone still cared.

❖ ❖ ❖

A phone call from my dad brought Gib's parents rushing over to our house. My fellow perpetrator and I gave our reluctant confession to a room full of somber adults, and even in my terror, as I faced the impending wrath of my father, I wondered if Gib would ever be my friend again.

I had crumbled. Sure, it was his mistake in the telling of his story that caused it, but I had caved in nonetheless.

And now we were in trouble. Big trouble.

❖ ❖ ❖

"We've examined the compromised stones and there doesn't appear to be any permanent damage. I don't believe any of them is broken, which is fortunate." Conrad stood in the doorway, still firmly gripping his hat with his nervous hands, talking with Dad and Stu Gillespie.

"So, what'll happen to the boys?" Stu calmly asked.

Maggie Gillespie was beside herself when she arrived at our haunted old house. She was filled with rage and embarrassment and ready, it seemed, to kill herself a couple of ten-year-old knuckleheads. But Stu, always the Rock of Gibralter, appeared unmoved by the raging storm that now threatened the tranquility of Rooster and the sanity of his wife.

"Well, I am going to recommend that the sheriff allow the two of you to split the cost of erecting and replacing the stones like you suggested, and remand the boys to your care. He may insist on sending them to a judge, but I doubt it."

"Good," said Dad. "When will we know?"

"Tomorrow. I'll call you, Reverend."

"Thank you."

"Try not to worry too much. It'll all work out." Then, he lowered his voice, thinking I would not be able to hear, "Just put the fear of God into them. Things like this can lead to much worse behavior with more serious consequences." Dad and Mr. Gillespie assured the deputy that this opportunity for teaching us a lesson would not be wasted.

Sure, the twelve licks Dad vigorously unleashed on my clinched backside with his forty-four inch black leather belt were painful. In fact, there were fleeting moments when my very survival was in doubt, at least in my mind. But, in retrospect, I would prefer Dad's twelve to Big Granddad's eight or ten any day.

Over the years, I became an authority on whippings. I even developed a ranking system, taking into account the instrument of punishment, the brute strength of the executioner, the number of licks given, and the ability of the executioner to hit the target. On a scale from "no sweat" to "say your prayers," Big Granddad, with his razor strap, ranked highest, or lowest, depending on your viewpoint. Dad and his long leather belt was a distant second, closely followed by Coach Scott's wooden paddle with the holes drilled in it. Mom's flyswatter on the naked behind was a surprising and most unpleasant fourth, but Gramma's rolled-up newspaper barely registered.

CHAPTER 5

Unconditional Love...And Other Strange Dreams

Despite Deputy Joe Conrad's brilliant portrayal of Dr. Seuss' Grinch, Christmas did come to the Reynolds household in 1971, right on time, and just two weeks after the day I entered the criminal ranks in the Rooster cemetery.

I was filled with a strange mixture of anticipation and dread as I sat cross-legged on the living room floor, watching Rachel open her first gift.

"Oh, Mommy! It's just what I wanted," she squealed as she tore the last bit of wrapping paper off her new baby buggy. She leaped to her feet, ran first to Mom, then to Dad, planting a big kiss on each of their cheeks, and hugging their necks.

That scene was repeated again and again as she opened each successive gift. A new baby doll. Squeal, kiss, kiss. Baby doll clothes. Squeal, kiss, kiss. Baby bottle and pacifier. Squeal, kiss, kiss.

She got everything she asked for. Everything! But then, she never wrecked a graveyard, either. Her worst transgression was refusing to eat her peas. Of course she would get what she wished for.

But, not me. No way. Not only had I done a terrible, terrible thing. I had chosen the worst possible time to do it.

I knew Santa wasn't going to bring me anything. He never did. In fact, not once did he ever even so much as stop at our house. Mom and Dad taught us that Santa Claus was just a myth. It was fun to pretend he was real. It was fun to go to the JC Penney in downtown Fort Worth and sit in his lap and tell him what you want for Christmas. But all that was just pretend.

Santa was a myth. Jesus was real. That's what we were taught. That is what we believed, Rachel and me.

And that was OK with me. I did just fine without the jolly elf. Mom and Dad always saw to it that we had a great Christmas.

It was our family tradition to have a big dinner on Christmas Eve, complete with Dad's and my favorite dessert, pecan pie. (That year, the pecans had come from our own tree!) Then we would all sit on the living room floor in front of our grand Christmas tree. Dad would take his big black bible and read the Christmas story from the gospels of Matthew and Luke. How I loved that story of Joseph and Mary and baby Jesus. The angels singing to lowly shepherds in a lonely field. The wise men in their royal garments, bearing precious gifts. The wicked, bloodthirsty King Herod and his determination to stamp out Christmas before it even got started. To me, it was Christmas magic.

Then Dad would close his bible, we would all hold hands and he would pray. Oh, how he would pray.

When my dad prayed I imagined that all the harps in heaven were silenced, the angels would stop flapping their wings, the choirs would hush their singing...all so God could hear the prayer of Daniel Reynolds.

But that Christmas I didn't hear my dad's prayer. My mind was preoccupied with the dreadful thought that I would receive no presents. Why should I? Because of me our family and church were the scourge of Rooster. Prank callers kept dialing our number, making sounds like ghosts and whispering things like, "You have disturbed my sleep, now you must pay." Some vandals had even spray-painted the word "GRAVEROBBERS" on the front door of our church.

Calvary Baptist Church was one of only five churches in town. There was St. Mary's Catholic Church, Rooster Church of Christ, First Methodist Church, First Baptist Church, and us. We were the smallest, least influential church in town. We were the "other" Baptist church, the one where all the misfits and outcasts attended. At least, that seemed to be the public perception.

And now we were harboring two known criminals. And one of them was the preacher's kid!

My dad had suffered two weeks of terrible embarrassment and humiliation. Everywhere he went people were giving him funny looks and sideways glances. Most gave him the cold shoulder. One or two said rude, hateful things to him.

Folks were angry and blaming my dad for his demon seed. They figured it all out for themselves. The Gillespies were good people, had been in the community for years. Sure, Gib was a handful. Ok, so he liked a good scrap and was a known cusser. But, he had never gotten himself into any real trouble to speak of.

At least, not until he came under the influence of that preacher's kid.

The whispers, the pointing fingers, the rumors were taking a toll on Dad. Just two nights before, I had heard him talking with Mom about it in their bedroom, and he was crying. I couldn't get that out of my head. I had made my dad, my wonderful, jolly dad cry.

Maybe I wouldn't go to Hell for it, or maybe I would. But one thing seemed certain. I dadgum sure wasn't gonna get any Christmas presents.

So, while Dad prayed, so did I. For forgiveness. For mercy. For an electric football game.

❦ ❦ ❦

Dad saw me squirming and sweating while Rachel reveled, and he just let me.

Finally, Rachel opened her last gift, gave out her last squeal, and completed her final victory lap, even stopping to kiss me.

Now it was my turn. Or was it? This was the moment of truth.

Mom paused, looking expectantly at Dad, who was enjoying the proceedings from his perch on our over-sized floral patterned couch.

"C'mere, son," Dad said, motioning to me. I walked sheepishly to him.

With his puffy hands on my shoulders, Dad said, "Son, your mother and I love you with all our hearts. And we forgive you for what you've done. Do you hear me? We love you."

"Y-yessir."

Tears trailed down Dad's face, rolling along the laugh lines in his cheeks, and merging at the dimple in his chin.

"Now, I hope you have learned a lesson and that you will think about the consequences of your actions from now on."

"Yes, sir," I mumbled, still painfully aware of a huge load of guilt, especially because of how Mom and Dad had been affected. I even noticed for the first time hints of gray in my dad's sideburns, and thought I must have put them there.

❦ ❦ ❦

Relieved that the tombstone incident was finally put to rest so far as my parents were concerned, and even more relieved that I would indeed have Christmas like everyone else, I happily returned to my place on the floor, directly in front of our Christmas tree.

Mom sighed with obvious relief, smiling her angelic smile, and bent to kiss me gently on the cheek. She stroked my hair with her hand and whispered, "I love you, Reginald."

Then Momma Claus handed me my first gift. It was wrapped in the silver and gold angel paper and was obviously some type of clothing. But I didn't care. It was a present, by golly! It was *my* present. I lustily tore into the defenseless angels, ripping paper and tossing it aside until I was left with a white box, securely taped about the edges. (Mom had a habit of taping the boxes as if whatever was inside might escape.) I was too anxious to tear at each piece of Scotch tape. Instead, I just ripped the lid in two, extracting a gasp from my mom, who insisted on saving all boxes and bows for future use.

I pulled from the mangled package a Dallas Cowboys football jersey with the number 12 proudly displayed on the back.

"Aw, man!" I said, "Roger Staubach! Cool!"

I ripped the shirt I was wearing off and, before Mom could protest, slipped my new treasure over my head.

That Christmas I received the best haul ever. An official NFL football and kicking tee. Cleats. A Dallas Cowboys helmet. And last and greatest of all—the latest, state-of-the-art electric football game, complete with all twenty-six teams.

❧ ❧ ❧

Christmas 1971 remains to this day the best Christmas of my life. I have received bigger and more costly gifts, to be sure. But none more meaningful.

That year I received the gift of unconditional love. I had learned a lesson about what Dad called "unmerited favor" in his sermons.

In my bed that night I lay with my hands behind my head, and engaged in my very first unprompted serious conversation with God.

"Dear Jesus," I prayed, "If you love me even better than my parents do, then your love must be the greatest thing in the whole world." And then, to emphasize my sincerity, I slipped from my bed and knelt beside it, folding my hands beneath my chin and said, "Lord Jesus, I will do anything you want me to do. Anything. Amen."

That night I dreamed my dad had died. I was standing all alone in front of his tombstone which, oddly enough, looked just like Robert Orrin James' marker.

There was someone else standing beside me. He looked like Big Granddad, but I knew it was God. And then he spoke to me.

"Reg," God said, "I want you to finish the job he started."

"What? What do you mean? What job, Lord?"

"I want you to be a preacher of the Gospel, son."

"I c-can't. I'm just a boy."

"Of course you can. And you must. I have chosen you and I will be with you. You are more than a mere boy," God said, "You are my child. Go. Preach."

"Yessir," I answered.

I awakened to the darkness and silence of my upstairs bedroom, listening for awhile to the slapping of sleet against the window. Then I slipped from bed and crept down the stairs to my parents' bedroom.

Through the door I could hear the heavy breathing of my mother as she slept. But my dad's familiar snore was not there.

I pressed my ear to the door to see if I could hear him breathing.

Nothing!

Panic-stricken, I twisted the brass doorknob, lunged against the door and burst into my parents' room. Mom shuffled in the bed, but did not awaken.

"Dad!" I tried to yell, but could only whisper, as mortal fear gripped my throat, paralyzing my vocal cord.

He was not there.

Mom snorted. "What, what" she said, in her sleep.

"Dad! Where's my dad?" I pleaded in a horse whisper, though I was trying to yell.

Just then, a strong and familiar hand gripped my shoulder.

"Son, what is it?"

I wheeled about to face the silhouette of my father against the dim glow of Christmas tree lights.

"Dad," I cried, "I had a dream. I thought you were dead." Then I wrapped my arms around his barrel waist and buried my face in his chest.

"It's alright, my boy," Dad said, cupping my head in his hands. "It was only a dream. I am fine. Everyone is fine. It was only a dream."

❧ ❧ ❧

Christmas night, my Uncle Roy Henderson and I lay in the twin beds in his room. He was unusually quiet and attentive as I rehearsed for him the dream I had suffered the night before.

As was our custom, my family and I had arisen early Christmas morning to the smell of bacon and coffee. Mom always beat everyone else out of bed, and by the time we were dressed, breakfast—bacon and eggs, biscuits and gravy, coffee and juice—was on the table.

After breakfast we loaded the gifts we had bought for Big Granddad and Gramma in Mom's chocolate brown Cadillac, and headed for Mineral Wells to celebrate Christmas with the extended family.

Ordinarily, Roy would make some wisecrack. Or, he would have tried to sell me a line about the meaning of my dream, and then secretly delighted in my mental torture. He was a world-class prankster. And I was his favorite and most frequent victim. Sometimes, I sniffed out his traps, but usually played ignorant anyway. I don't know why I always let him win these mind games. I guess I just accepted it as my role. He was the prankster; I was the target. That was the order of things.

Still I admired and loved Roy. He seemed to be everything I wanted to be. He was smart, good-looking, popular in school, and a great athlete. He and I and the other boys in Big Granddad's church spent many a happy hour playing football or flies and skinners in the empty lot next to the church.

Roy rolled over on his side propping his head up on his hand. I could tell he was straining to see me better in the darkness. Obviously, my dream was a subject that had piqued his interest.

"So, God spoke to you in a dream?"

"Yeah."

"And He told you that He wanted you to preach?"

"Sure did."

Silence.

"Roy?"

"What?"

"Has God ever spoken to you?"

"Once."

"When?"

"Last night. In a dream."

Roy was in earnest contemplation. He was not his usual playful, ornery self at all. This coincidence of simultaneous dreams had his full concentration.

"Roy, what did God say to you?"

"He told me He wanted me to preach."

"Wow!" I whispered hoarsely, feeling a sudden chill up my spine. "That's weird."

"Sure is."

Nothing more was said. I lay there in the darkness and listened to the muffled conversation and laughter of the adults, who were in the dining room, playing forty-two. Soon I was sound asleep with nary a dream in my head.

CHAPTER 6

Fighting Back

Gib was not as fortunate as I. His parents decided the best way to teach their little criminal a lasting lesson was to withhold any and all Christmas presents from him. In their eyes, it was only just. In Gib's eyes, and mine, it was cruel and unusual punishment.

Both sets of parents had agreed to keep Gib and me separated until school resumed. So, I was unaware that while I wrestled with the meaning of a strange dream and spent countless hours playing with my electric football game, Gib was seething, vowing to get even with that no-good drunken snitch, Rufe Jones and his brood of ill-kempt, uncivilized kids.

Rufe Jones was the town drunk. He always sported a stubble of beard and wore his hair heavily greased and slicked back, usually with a few matted strands falling into his face. He was of an average build, somewhere in his mid-to-late fifties. His hair was jet black. His skin tanned and rough.

I had shaken his hand once when he visited our church on a Sunday morning, after an all-night drinking binge. I remember his blood-shot eyes, liquored breath, yellowed teeth, and hardened hands. Shaking his hand was like grabbing a log for the fireplace. It was rough and hard and big and strong.

Legend had it that Rufe had once been one of Rooster's upstanding citizens. He had worked in the City National Bank as a loan officer, which made him an extremely important person about town, since there was only one bank, and it had only one loan officer.

But sometime in the early 1960's Rufe's wife, a woman of extraordinary beauty, engaged in an illicit affair with the pastor of the First Baptist Church. Rufe discovered them in his bedroom one day and proceeded to beat the both of them with a tire tool. The preacher was rendered unconscious from the beating, suffering a fractured skull, broken nose and teeth and several busted ribs. He was forced to leave the town and the ministry, and he was never heard from in those parts again.

Elizabeth, Rufe's wife, faired no better. She was terribly beaten, bruised and scarred by the savage attack of her crazed husband. She lost the use of her left eye and her leg was so badly twisted that she walked with a limp for the rest of her life—which wasn't long, since, unable to deal with the shame of her actions and the fear of her husband, she placed Rufe's Colt .45 revolver in her mouth just two years later and splattered her brains and bits of skull all over the kitchen wall.

Rufe spent six years in the state penitentiary in Huntsville on charges of assault and attempted murder. While he was in there, he choked the life from a man who had allegedly attempted to sexually assault him in the shower. The incident was ruled self-defense and he received no additional sentence.

Rufe's old mother took in the Jones kids while he was in prison. She was nearly ninety, senile and legally blind, and the five kids were pretty much left to fend for themselves. Consequently, the two girls and two oldest boys were an unruly lot. They engaged in petty thievery, vandalism, fistfights and whatever other forms of mischief their limited minds could conceive. Most people just steered clear of them, and instructed their children to do the same.

The youngest of the four, Patrick, was just a baby when his Momma died and his daddy went off to prison. And in 1971–72, he was a member of Mrs. Konnerup's fifth grade class.

❧ ❧ ❧

Most kids hated going back to school after Christmas break, and ordinarily I would have been among them. But not my fifth grade year.

For me the resumption of school meant two very exciting things were about to happen. My grounding from my best friend Gib was being lifted. And I would see that angelic creature whose every feature was etched indelibly in my mind, Lori Anne Golden.

❧ ❧ ❧

"Pssst. Hey, Preach!" Gib whispered from behind me as we stood next to the blackboard, waiting our turn to sharpen our pencils. "You comin' over today?"

"Yeah," I exulted, in something just above a whisper. Ms. Konnerup shot me a stern glance from over her reading glasses, and placed her index finger over her lips to quieten me.

"Good! 'Cause I'm gonna need some backup."

"Backup? What are you talk…"

"Gentlemen! Return to your seats this instant." Mrs. Konnerup was standing behind her desk, hands on her hips, looking like a Mount Rushmore figure. I was left to wonder what in the world my friend meant about needing backup.

❧ ❧ ❧

At first recess, I learned exactly what Gib meant. He had no interest in games of kickball or kill-the-man-with-the-ball or foot-racing. Instead, he made a beeline for the one boy in the fifth-grade class I had never seen him threaten, challenge, or even acknowledge the existence of. Patrick Jones.

No one messed with Patrick. He was an ugly kid, a misfit, who always seemed to have crusty, dried-up snot under his nose. He usually reeked of some ungodly mixture of sweat and urine. His clothes were seldom clean and it is doubtful he took more than a bath a week.

Patrick was quiet. Really quiet. Half the school year had already elapsed and I had yet to hear him utter a sentence without a direct order accompanied by threats from Ms. Konnerup. During recess, he went around to the side of the school and doodled in the dirt, or just leaned against the building, staring blankly at the rest of us playing on the schoolyard.

Ms. Konnerup had tried on several occasions to force the other boys in the class to include Patrick in our games. But we ignored her directives.

"The kid's a damn retard," Gib complained once. He was sent directly to Principal Railey's office for cussing and having a general bad attitude. Three licks with Railey's holey paddle did nothing to change his opinion.

Gib marched up to Patrick Jones, who was squatted down beside the school building, tormenting a doodlebug with a stick. When Patrick saw Gib approaching and Chuck Illich and Willy Hernandez and me following closely behind, he dropped his stick and stood up, brushing the dirt from his hands on his pants.

Gib stopped only when he was literally nose to nose with the outcast. "Listen, you damn retard. Your dad is a stinking drunk and a lousy snitch, your dead Momma was a tramp and you smell worse than a commode fulla shit! Whattaya think about that?"

Patrick said nothing. He just shoved his hands into his pockets and made a snorting sound, blowing a snot bubble out of his left nostril.

Gib jumped back, wiping the kid's snot from the tip of his own nose. "Sonuvabi…I oughtta…You just wait, 'tard. After school! After school!" Gib was waving his finger in Patrick's direction as he walked back towards the classroom. Patrick still didn't utter a word. He just stuck out his tongue and made a long, gross farting sound with his mouth.

Poor kid. Doesn't even know he's dead.

❧ ❧ ❧

The rest of the day was a waste so far as learning was concerned, at least for me it was. I had seen a side of my friend that I didn't much like. It didn't bother me at all that he loved to pick fights. I was proud of him, in fact. I wished I were a tough guy like Gib.

But this was different. Gib's other conquests had been at the expense of "normal" kids, kids who had all their marbles. Gib was more gallant than this. He was an agitator. But he was no bully. He never preyed on the weak. That would be no sport at all.

But he was smarting over a lost Christmas and a miserable school holiday. In his mind, someone had to pay. And that someone was the one who ratted us out. Rufus Jones. But Gib was a realist. He could do nothing to get even with Rufus. The mean old drunk would make short work of him, just like he had that preacher, and the prisoner, and his own wife.

Gib would not entertain the thought of something as anonymous and cheap as vandalizing the Jones' homestead. Besides, it was such a pigsty they probably wouldn't even notice. The next best thing would be to whup his kid. And that is just what Gilbert Gillespie determined to do. There might not be much sport in it. But there would be satisfaction.

❧ ❧ ❧

Ms. Konnerup had caught wind of Gib's scheme and determined to put a stop to it. However, she didn't want to get her pupil in any more trouble at home. So, she kept Gib and me in class for fifteen minutes after the last bell rang, figuring that would give Patrick ample time to get home.

The Kernel took the opportunity to lecture us. "You know, gentlemen, fighting doesn't solve anything. Gib, even if you beat Patrick up, would that change what happened? Would it make it better? Or worse? You need to learn to forgive and forget the past." Konnerup was sounding like a preacher! "You brought this on yourselves. It's no one's fault but your own. But, you need to forgive yourself, too. Life goes on. You live and you learn."

Her words made perfect sense to me, and I hoped Gib would heed them. But, looking into his eyes, I knew better. He would not be deterred.

My stubborn friend folded his arms and stared defiantly ahead.

❧ ❧ ❧

When Konnerup finally released us, Gib set out to follow Patrick's usual path home. He knew it because the Jones' house was in the same direction as his, just a couple of streets further.

Along the way, Chuck and Willy fell in with us. We turned onto Strawn Street, and passed directly in front of the Golden residence. Lori Anne saw us from her living room window and ran through the screen door, bounding down the steps and across the lawn. I was immediately distracted from the task at hand, as I suddenly found myself standing face to face with the only girl in the whole world I was interested in. Interested, heck! I was smitten. I wanted to impress her. I wanted to be witty and charming and funny and everything she could possibly want in a man. Instead, I was mostly tongue-tied.

"Hi, guys," said Lori, who turned to walk along with us, right between me and Gib. Not a single boy protested her presence, either. "Where are we going?"

"Lookin' for a retard," said Gib, who seemed not the least interested in the fact that he was in the presence of an angelic being.

"Oh, puh-lease! You don't really intend to fight that poor boy, Gilbert."

"Durn sure do! An' if ya don't like it, best get home." Gib shot her a menacing glance for emphasis.

"C'mon, Gib!" said I before I could stop myself, "She hasn't done anything to you. Leave her alone."

I braced myself for Gib's assault, fully expecting him to whirl about and commence to beating the living crap out of me. But he didn't. He ignored my defense of Lori and quickened his pace.

We walked in silence until we came to the Gillespie residence, then we turned into the alley across the street from their driveway and followed the known shortcut to Patrick's house.

Along the dirt path there were three houses, two on the north side and one on the south. These houses faced gravel roads that ran parallel to the alley. They all had chain-link fences, the backs of which lined the alley. In the fence on the south there were three big, mean German Shepherd dogs, which we had occasionally tormented with rocks, B-B guns and sticks. As soon as we turned into the alley the dogs went crazy, barking and growling and bearing their teeth, running up and down the fence line, looking for a way to get at us.

Without a word, we all veered to the left to get as far from the fenced beasts as possible. When we walked under the big oak tree that stood next to the fence of the second house on the north side, we heard a blood-curdling scream that brought to mind the war cry of the Apache Indians in the Louis L'Amour novels my dad loved to read. The scream erupted from directly above us, somewhere in the branches of the big oak tree. We all froze in our tracks and looked up. Out of my peripheral vision I caught a blur. Something was hurled directly at Gib.

It was Patrick Jones who had launched himself from a low limb of the old tree. He caught Gib with both knees between the shoulder blades, sending my friend sprawling, landing face down on the hard-packed earth. The wind knocked out of him, Gib lay spread-eagle on the ground for several seconds, unable to move.

Patrick, who could not control his fall after colliding with Gib, fell solidly on his tailbone, his head jerking forward, smashing his face into his right knee. Stunned by the vicious blow to the bridge of his nose, Patrick groaned and rolled over onto his knees and elbows, resting his head against the ground.

"Chit, man!" said Wee Willy.

"Hey! Gib," said I kneeling down beside him, "You okay?"

"Course…I…am," Gib wheezed, "Just leave…me…alone." He waved me off, and then pulled himself up, resting a minute on his hands and knees. Gib had a mouthful of dirt. He struggled to sit upright on his knees, wiping the mud from his mouth onto his shirtsleeve.

Lori was on her knees beside Patrick Jones, trying to tend to him, but he growled and shoved her away.

Gib was the first of the combatants to reach his feet. When he did, he moved quickly toward his opponent, hell-bent on beating him to a bloody pulp. As he had done earlier at the school, Patrick Jones shoved his hands into his pockets and stared blankly at his assailant. Gib was taking his final quick step with his left foot and cocking his right one to kick the Jones kid full in the face, when the strange boy, letting out another shrill war cry, lunged forward, pulling his hand from his jeans pocket and swinging a wide arc towards Gib's throat. Patrick was surprisingly quick and his counterattack caught Gib completely off guard.

I saw the glimmer of something metal in Patrick's clenched right fist.

"My God!" I shouted "Gib, he's got a knife."

Quick as Patrick Jones was, Gilbert Gillespie was quicker. He managed to duck the weapon aimed at his throat, catching it along his left cheekbone instead. Missing his mark and unable to control his momentum, Patrick spun halfway around, falling to one knee. Gib, blood gushing from his short, but to-the-bone wound, grabbed a handful of Patrick's hair and jerked his head downward as he shot his own knee upward. The jarring blow caught Patrick in his right eye. His head flopped backward and he toppled over onto his back. Gib leaped onto his fallen opponent, pinning Patrick's arms with his knees and sitting on his chest. He grabbed the fallen warrior by each ear, and commenced to banging his head against the ground.

"You...tell...your...drunk...daddy...he...caused...this," Gib screamed, as he tried to crack Patrick's head like an egg.

Chuck Illich and I grabbed our friend by his arms and dragged him from his prey. The Jones boy was still conscious, but unable to resist the vicious assault. The fight was over.

Gib clawed and scratched at us as we struggled mightily to restrain him. The fingernails of his left hand dug deep into the skin of my forearm, leaving bloody skidmarks and resulting in three short but distinct scars that today look rather like white war-paint on my right arm, halfway between my wrist and elbow.

Finally, the tempest in Gilbert Gillespie's mind subsided. He wrestled free from our grip, picking up the shiny weapon that had been intended to decapitate him. It wasn't a knife at all, but an old can opener, bent to a right angle from the impact with Gib's cheekbone.

Gilbert walked over to where Patrick still lay prone on the ground, chest heaving with exhaustion, gurgling on the blood that was draining from his busted nose into his throat. My friend knelt beside the kid he had just tried to destroy.

"Sorry, kid." Gib lay the can opener on the heaving chest of Patrick Jones. "You fight real good."

With that, Gilbert Gillespie stood up on wobbly legs and, without another word, walked slowly home. He would have to be taken by his mother to Ranger to the Hospital there so he could receive seven stitches in his left cheekbone, just inches below his eye, and a Tetanus shot in his clenched butt. Mrs. Gillespie railed on her warrior-son the whole fifteen miles there and back. "It's a wonder that boy din't put yer eye out, Gilbert Gillespie. An' it would be good enough for ye, too if he had! What am I gonna do with you? What's it gonna take? You won't be satisfied 'til I'm a childless mother, or else ye put me in th' grave m'self." These and assorted other admonitions streamed non-stop both legs of the trip that resulted in Gib's getting the stitches that helped to seal his claim as the toughest, meanest hombre in the whole damn fifth grade.

I watched Gib walk away from the battlefield, my faith in him restored because of his magnanimous gesture towards his vanquished foe. Only then did I hear what an awful noise those killer dogs were making, obviously feeling jilted because they couldn't participate in the carnage. The dogs' owner was yelling and kicking at them and beating them with the belt he had just pulled from his greasy blue work pants.

The dogs retreated from their abusive master, leaving him free to address us, which he did.

"Whut the hell you younguns a doin back here?" The shirtless, pot-bellied grease monkey growled, waving a half-empty can of Blue Ribbon beer at us.

"Now, you just cut that brawlin' out and get on up outta here, afore I turn these hounds loose on yer asses. G'wan now. Git!"

Not wanting to attract the attention of any responsible adults, we immediately decided it was time to get out of there. Lori and I helped Patrick to his feet, ignoring his attempts to push us away, and pointed him in the direction of his house.

"Can you make it home?" Lori asked softly. Patrick sucked the stream of blood and snot back into his nose, grunted, pulling himself free from her grip, and stumbled down the alley towards his house.

Willy and Chuck were already headed up the alley. They had to hurry home or else answer all kinds of questions about where they'd been.

That left only me to escort Lori Anne Golden home.

Lucky me.

CHAPTER 7

Sudden Death

I was daydreaming. From my desk on the back row I stared across the fifth grade classroom, out the window, into the world. I watched a bright red Cardinal perched on the branch of a pear tree. If I only had my pellet gun—the one that if pumped as many as ten times had the velocity of a .22, by gosh—I would make short work of that proud bird and his tail feather would adorn the band of my cowboy hat sitting atop my dresser at home. Somewhere in the background I could hear Ms. Konnerup drone on about what a great year it had been and how fond she was of all of us and, sniff, would we please not forget her, and sometime next year stop to say hi.

Ah, the last day of school! The Twenty-Sixth of May. The sun is shining. The birds are singing. And soon the final bell will ring on my fifth grade year. Free at last! Free to hike to Rooster Lake, which is hardly a lake at all, more of a glorified pond, but who cares? The water is cold and deep and Gib says there's a secret swimmin' hole that he discovered last Summer that no one else in the whole damn town or county for that matter knows about. He says it's not a stone's throw from the famous spot where Roy Orrin James caught and killed all four members of the notorious Porterhouse gang, who had robbed the town bank, shooting the teller to death. It was a glorious gunfight. Roy was wounded, shot through the shoulder, but he managed to kill all four of the bad guys. He was hell with a gun, as everyone knows. And since Roy doubled as the Baptist preacher and the town sheriff he was also the one who performed the funeral ceremony for the outlaws. Legend has it he took for his text the verse that says, "The soul that sinneth it shall die." And he committed their no-'count bodies to the grave and their sorry souls to Hell where they belonged and where he sent them. People say the next Lord's Day the gun-slingin' preacher waxed so eloquent on the wages of sin that more'n a hundred people streamed to the altar to beg God for salvation and that afternoon, in spite of his sore shoulder, he baptized them all not thirty yards from where he mowed down the Porterhouse boys.

With such things crowding my mind how could I concentrate or give any weight to the words of Ms. Konnerup, even if I had grown fond of her, too?

* * *

The grueling hours pass and the bell rings at last. What a beautiful sound! *Brrrrrrrrrinnnnnng.* School's out for the summer. Gib whoops and Philsbury hollers and we all make a mad dash for the door that has held us prisoner for nine months.

Into the glorious sunlight we run. Everyone is talking at once and no one is listening at all. Lori's going to spend the summer swimming and jumping on the trampoline. Chuck Illich is going to Dr. J's basketball camp all the way in Philadelphia where his aunt and uncle live and where Julius Erving is both king and jester on the basketball court. Wee Willy is going all the way to some town in Mexico, which I can't pronounce, or spell but I know is near Mexico City and where Gib says he belongs, the damn Chalupa. Gib and I will go to Rooster Lake. We will swim, fish, hunt, explore and reenact the fine day when Ol' Roy whupped the Porterhouse gang and whupped 'em good. Phil Farmer isn't going anywhere, well, except to work with his dad driving a semi every other week or so, and he would like to come with Gib and me. And Gib says maybe, but we'll have to think about it. Phil he knows would slow us down because he's fat and slow of foot. But he would be great fun in the swimmin' hole. He can do the biggest baddest cannonball in Rooster. "And is it any wonder," says Gib, "With that lard ass hittin' the water from ten feet above."

I'm so excited about the last day of school I hardly notice that Lori Ann Golden is standing right before me trying to get my attention.

"Reg, are you listening to me?'

"Huh, wha—...oh yeah, sure. Sorry."

"Listen," she smiles, "I am really glad you came to our town and I had a really great time getting to know you. I hope we will see each other this summer."

"Yeah, me too."

"'Course you'll see him," Gib has invited himself into our private world, "How could ya miss that ugly mug in a town as small as this damn burg."

"Hush Gib. He's not ugly at all. He's sweet. Not like *some people* I know."

"Oooooh. Puppy love," says Chuck.

"Yeah," adds Gib, "But it's real to the dog!" He heard his Momma say that a few times and felt right proud that he was able to work such wonderful grownup wit into our conversation.

Kids are dispersing in all directions, headed home, anxious to get summer underway. Gib and Lori and I walk together in the direction of their houses and away from mine. Mom and Dad are off in Mineral Wells working at the car lot. Rachel is being babysat by Mrs. Norris, wife of the old deacon in our church, Ralph Norris, the one Gib calls a slack-jawed mouth-breather, because he always has his mouth gaping open like the hinge that holds it shut is worn out. Rachel loves it there because Mrs. Norris gives her a hot dog and a cookie and lets her watch Popeye the Sailor Man. So that means I get to spend the whole afternoon at Gib's. And when Mom and Dad come to get me we will beg them to let me spend the night. "Why not?" We'll reason, "It's summer. No school tomorrow!" And Mrs. Gillespie will say, "Ah, Pastor let him stay. He's no trouble a-tall and maybe he'll keep Gib outta mischief." And Dad will wink and say, "Steer clear of the dead and their dwellings, boys."

Gib and Lori and I are headed towards her house. Maybe we'll jump on the trampoline with her awhile before we go home, if, Gib insists, she promises not to bore the hell out of us with girl talk and other nonsense. And Lori elbows him and tells him, "Mind your manners and watch your tongue. I'm a lady, y'know." Gib says, "If you were a lady you'd have bigger…" And she whirls to face him, nose to nose. "Not another word, Gilbert Gillespie, or I'll forget myself." She learned that "forget myself" statement from her mom who sometimes forgets herself and says a dirty word or does some other unladylike thing and says, "I'm sorry, I forgot myself."

"Ok. Ok. Just foolin'. Don't be so touchy." So, the tension passes and I don't have to defend Lori's honor and confront my friend. Thank God. We walk on. Across the green grass of the school grounds and onto the bumpy roads of Rooster. When we get to the corner of Strawn Street, where Lori lives, we cut across an empty corner lot. The lot has not been given proper attention so in the places where grass still grows, it is nearly waste high, and the summer is hardly begun. But mostly the lot is just dirt and ragweed. There's an old 60 model Buick parked caddy-cornered across the lot. The wheels are gone from it. The trunk is missing and all the windows are smashed out from the rocks thrown at it over the years by kids like us.

* * *

Thump. Thump. I hear his big boots land on the hood of the Buick, one after the other before I look up to see him. Oh my God, he's big. And he has his hands on his hips and a great dip of Copenhagen in his lip. His nose is flat, pressed to his face, as if he has been run over by a train. He has stringy, dishwater blonde hair that clings to his forehead and sticks out over his ears from beneath his sweat-soaked John Deere cap. His denim overalls are baggy and dirty and he doesn't wear a shirt beneath them. He's a bit overweight, so his man breasts hang out on either side of his overall straps. There's a smattering of hairs on his white barrel chest. He's probably no more than six feet tall, but standing up on the hood of that car like that, he seems much bigger.

Jake Jones rakes the Copenhagen from his mouth with his fat finger, hurls it onto Gib's shoes and jumps off the car, landing right in front of Gib. He grabs a fistful of my friend's shirt and pulls him forward and up until he's standing on tiptoes. "You beat up the wrong kid, punk," he growls. "You shoulda thought who you was messin' wit' 'fore ya tore into my bruthuh."

"Hey, let him go!" *Is that my voice?* Yes, it is. "Let him go, ya big oaf. Pick on someone your own size. You're twice as big as Gib and prob'ly twice as old, though I doubt you're half as smart." Dad always said my smart mouth was going to get me in real trouble someday. *Shut up, Reg.*

"You, shuddup, if I need anythin from th' likes o' you, I'll knock it outta ya, little shit."

Then, there's someone clamping both of my arms behind my back, twisting them so that it hurts like crazy and I let out a howl. Two of Jake's dropout goon buddies are holding me. One of them snatches a handful of my hair and jerks my head back. "Say the word, Jake, and we'll break both his arms and legs."

"Just hold 'im. When I get through with this pissant I'll tend to the preacher boy."

I look at Gib there on his tiptoes and I think he is about to die. But it isn't fear I see in his eyes. It's rage. A black rage like he was in when he tried to crack poor Patrick's head like an egg. Gib harks a loogie and spits it in the face of the ugly giant. Square in the face! Jake yells, "Arrrggghhh," and whips Gib off the ground, whirls around and slams him into the driver side door of the Buick. The handle catches Gib somewhere in the ribs and I hear the air rush from his lungs. He looks sick. His eyes are filling with tears. The brute cocks his right hand across his own chest and unleashes a vicious backhand. His knuckles catch Gib full in the jaw and his knees buckle beneath him. When Jake loosens his grip on Gib's shirt, my friend slides to the ground, dazed, hurt, wheezing. I struggle against the restraints of my tormentors and they twist my arms and pull my hair even harder. And I am hurting and tears are coming to my eyes and I don't want to cry in front of Lori. That's for sure.

* * *

Jesse Gillespie turned eight May 25, 1972, the day before the last day of school. He got a brand new baseball, a baseball glove and a bat for his birthday. The next day he knew he would have a grand time because his big brother, Gib, promised him at his party, "Me an' Preach'll teach ya how to throw and catch and bat the ball tomorrow after school."

But he is tired of waiting for us to get home and decides to meet us along the way. We could toss the ball to him maybe on the way home. When he turns onto the vacant lot on the corner of Strawn and First Streets, he starts crying. His brother is in a heap on the ground beside the big brown car and some big monster in overalls has him by the hair, slamming his head into the door.

Jesse is mild-mannered, not given to frequent rages like his Mom and brother. He seldom gets very angry or upset, but when he does…Well, he's his father made over, so his Mom says. He will just go berserk, yelling, screaming uncontrollably. He could hurt himself or someone else if he isn't restrained. And he doesn't cool down quickly, either. It might take hours for him to return to a state of sanity.

Jesse is in a rage. I hear him scream. See him drop his glove with the baseball in it and run at Jake Jones. Jake looks around just in time to stop the bat with the bridge of his already flattened-out nose. Blood spurts like someone squashed a tomato on his face. He yelps, drops Gib, and falls back against the car. He is steadying himself, having dropped to one knee, when Jesse, still screaming something intangible cocks and swings the bat again. Jake throws up his left hand and the bat cracks against the bone of us his fleshy forearm. He yelps again, sounding like the little Chihuahua my sister got two Christmases ago, when the poor thing got his leg run over by a pickup back in Mineral Wells.

This time, though, the big kid catches the bat, jerks it away from little Jesse and shoves him hard to the ground. Jesse bounces back like a rubber ball, head down, and charges into Jake again, his short brown arms flailing wildly. Jake leaps to his feet, swinging the bat, like Babe Ruth in overalls, at the young hellion.

The thud is sickening. You can hear it cracking bone and sinking into soft tissue. Jake has nailed my friend's kid brother in the left temporal. Blood splatters and is slung from the end of the bat, some of it hitting me in the face and neck, ten feet away. Like a slow-motion replay on the Sunday football game I see it. Jesse's head snaps to the right. He stops mid-stride. And he stands there. He is looking right at me, a blank stare on his face. And then his eyes roll up in his head and he falls straightforward to the ground. He is laying on his stomach, both arms trapped beneath his body, head cocked to the side in a weird way, his eyes wide open with only the whites of them showing. And his tongue is hanging out.

His body jerks three or four times, a gush of air escapes through his mouth kicking up a little cloud of dirt. And then he is still.

The blood and dirt commingle around young Jesse's head to form a dark maroon, muddy pool. Big Jake stands above the boy, the bat, wet with his and Jesse's blood still clenched in his two fists. He sways to the right and then to the left, back and forth and looks as if he might pass out. Then he lifts the bat again.

Sometime in these seconds that seem like hours my two captors have turned me loose and are high-tailing it out of there. Realizing I'm free and thinking Jake is about to finish the job on young Jesse's head, I grab the baseball that had rolled from Jesse's glove, turn and, with my strong left arm that has helped me earn all-star honors as a Little League pitcher, fire a fastball. It's a strike. Jake never sees it coming. Square in the forehead the ball hits him. His head snaps backward and the ball shoots forward, like a pop fly. I snag the fly and fire again this time at almost point blank range. He catches it with his mouth, which is still agape from the shock of the first blow. I hear teeth crunch and a sound like that of a plunger unstopping a commode. The ball sticks in his mouth. A picture I once saw of a Hawaiian Luau flashes across my mind. A pig with an apple in his mouth—I guess because he is a big fat kid and the ball is red with the blood of his forehead, mouth and busted nose.

Jake Jones sways like a tall tree in a strong West Texas wind. Forward and back, side to side he sways. And then he topples and tumbles to the ground. David fells Goliath with a fastball.

When Lori saw Jake Jones, one of the town's biggest thugs, grab poor Gib by the shirt, she knew something bad would happen. And then Jake's only two friends in the world, the Bandy twins, Billy and Bobby, grabbed me from behind and started twisting my arms and pulling my hair. These high school dropouts were all seventeen years old, big and mean. She knew she had better do something and quick.

So she took off running. Lori didn't run like most girls. She could really move, gracefully and swiftly. She ran across the Bannisters' lawn and the Morris's and the Copperfields' to her own house.

"Mom, call Deputy Conrad and come quickly. Gib and Reg are in trouble."

Her mom tried to get her to explain the situation, but Lori insisted there was no time. She had to hurry or the boys might be hurt real bad or even killed. Hurry. Hurry.

Mrs. Golden called the sheriff's department and they promised to locate and dispatch Deputy Conrad as quickly as possible. And then she was out the door, chasing after Lori up Strawn Street towards the abandoned corner lot.

❧ ❧ ❧

"Oh my God!" I hear the high-pitched squeal of Mrs. Golden's voice. I am wiping Jesse's blood and my own sweat from my forehead, wondering if I killed the big punk, Jake Jones.

Mrs. Golden is on her knees, holding young Jesse's head in her hands. She has turned white and I think she is going to faint. Instead, she gently lays his head back into Gib's lap, who is sitting cross-legged on the ground holding his baby brother in his arms, crying, "Jesse. Jesse. Please. Wake up. Wake up. Oh, Jesse. Wake up."

"Don't move him, I am going to call Doctor White." And Mrs. Golden is up and running across the lot, but here comes Mr. Copperfield to see what all the fuss is about and she yells to him, "Joe, run and call Doctor White. Tell him it's an extreme emergency. He must come now. Jesse Gillespie is seriously injured. Hurry. Please, hurry."

Mr. Copperfield, who is only in his twenties and in very good physical condition, sprints to his house to call Doc White. The phone is busy, so he jumps in his car and races across town to the doctor's office.

Gib is bawling, snot running from his nose, mixing with the blood from the cuts on his forehead, nose and cheeks from Jake slamming him into the car door over and over. He's holding Jesse. Mrs. Golden is hugging him and Jesse and wiping Jesse's forehead and stroking his hair with her lovely soft hands. Lori and I are standing perfectly still, hardly breathing, staring at our friend's kid brother. And Jake, who isn't Goliath at all and isn't dead either, is sitting on his butt beside the old Buick, his knees pulled up to his chest and his hands locked under his knees. He's crying too and sounding like Whistlebritches, Rachel's dead Chihuahua again, saying, "I'm sorry. Oh Gawd, I'm sorry. I'm so sorry." And then he spits a bloody gob on the ground that contains one of his two front teeth and a piece of the other.

Here comes Mrs. Gillespie. She runs like Gib, all elbows and knees, her skirt flying up, showing her slip and even her drawers at times. She hits her knees and skids to a stop where her poor Jesse is laying in his brother's arms, both boys covered in blood. Mrs. Golden scoots out of the way and Maggie Gillespie takes Jesse and pulls him to her bosom. She isn't saying anything. I have never seen her not say anything. She isn't crying, looking wild in the eye or anything I expect. She is the picture of calm. She holds her little son so gently to herself and rocks him like he's back at home and still a baby. She is humming something sweet and then whispering softly in his ear. She pulls Gib to her and he buries his head in her shoulder and shakes bodily and bawls. He's sorry. He's so sorry. And Jake says he's sorry. "Oh Gawd, so very sorry." And, "What have I did? Gawd help me. What have I did?"

Here comes Doc White. "Ok, everyone, please move aside so I can look at this young man." Mrs. Gillespie doesn't move. She holds Jesse tightly to her bosom. Kisses him on his forehead. "You're too late, Doc. Too late. My fine boy is gone home to God." Now Gib is screaming and kicking Jake all about the face and chest. Jake doesn't lift a hand to defend himself. He just rocks back and forth on his butt and yelps like Whistlebritches. I grab Gib and pull him away from the big oaf. I am holding him as tightly as I can. "Gib, it's me. It's Reg. Gib." Then he crumples to the ground and bawls more violently than ever. Lori is on her knees beside him and so is Mrs. Golden and they're saying, "There, there. It isn't your fault. Gib. We love you. Everything is going to be alright." But it isn't. I know that much.

Doctor White has finally wrestled poor Jesse from his mother. He lays him on the blanket Mr. Copperfield has spread on the ground. Doc White works feverishly on the olive-skinned boy whose eyes are still open and rolled up in his head. He tries every way he knows to resuscitate him. He works and He works, this tall, gray-headed distinguished-looking gentleman from South Carolina. Great beads of sweat gather on his brow and he wipes them with a hanky from his pants pocket. Finally, with his thumb and forefinger he closes Jesse's eyes, pulls a little pad and pen from his white shirt pocket, which is now caked with blood and dirt, and records the time of death.

He hugs and comforts Mrs. Gillespie, whose silent tears are pouring down her face in such a stream that one would wonder how many tears a body contains. "I'll take Jesse with me, Mrs. Gillespie and get him cleaned up. I'll call Carl, too. Now, don't you worry m'lady, everything's going to be alright. God will take of your fair son, I know he will." Carl Underwood is the town's only mortician. He owns Underwood's Funeral Home and is one of Rooster's leading citizens, a deacon at the First Methodist Church, and president of the local chapter of the Lion's Club.

Mrs. Gillespie walks over to where Jake is still sitting, swaying and whimpering. Her voice is steady, not raised, unquivering. "Your soul will rot in Hell with that of your harlot mother an' drunken father some day. And that's too good for the likes of ye."

Then she takes Gib by the hand, tells me to c'mon and we walk across the abandoned corner lot to Strawn Street and on home.

There are very few brick homes in Rooster, Texas. And the Gillespie residence certainly is not one of them. It sits at the end of Third Street, right at the bottom of a little hill. It is the only house in the fifth block on the north side of Third. An unnamed dirt road runs alongside it, curving around into Second Street. The house seemed quite ample to me in 1972, though it is only a total of five rooms and one hallway. It has, of course, a big front porch, which is fronted by a stone ledge. At the far end there is a gaping hole in the boards of the porch, which Maggie Gillespie said Stu was fixin' to fix one day soon. Never mind the hole had already been there eight years or so. The old house was on pier and beam and the floors sagged and swayed, which made the front door stick so that it was all a ten year old boy, going on eleven could do to open it. The screen door was only screened on the bottom half. Those blasted house apes of hers had torn the rest away, said Mrs. Gillespie.

The front room was the living room where the family spent most of the time, because there was a good air conditioning unit in the east window. The two bedrooms were at either end of the hall on the west side of the house and the bathroom was in the middle of that hallway. Each bedroom had a swamp cooler in the window, but with the humidity it didn't do much good, just mostly made the hot air feel sticky to boot. Gib said in the heat of the summer he was the only kid in town with a sauna in his bedroom, though I doubted he'd ever seen a sauna. The kitchen was at the back of the house. It was so small that they could only fit a table scarcely bigger than a card table in there for family dining. Maybe that's why they had their kids in batches.

The Gillespies were a bit older than my parents, though their two boys, Gib and Jake, were about the same age of my sister and me. This was their second batch of kids. They had a son, Eugene and a daughter, Doreen, who were both in their twenties and both living somewhere in south Texas—anywhere but Rooster, said Gib.

We sat in Gib's room, Gib, Lori Anne, Chuck, Willy and me. Through the closed door we could hear the muffled voices of our parents as they talked in hushed tones about the day's events.

"That was a beautiful service, Reverend," I heard Mrs. Golden say. The Goldens, to my chagrin, were Methodists. They had attended our church only once on a special occasion and Mr. Golden had said ever since what a fine "orator" my father was—which I was sure was quite a high compliment but not exactly sure how. George Golden was a bronze statue...or at least he could have been. Parents were not supposed to look as fine as Lori Anne's did. Her dad was at least six-foot-two. He had chiseled features, a thin waist, sandy, neatly-groomed hair and a...well, a golden tan, just like Lori Anne. Brenda Golden, Lori Anne's mom was petite, thin, elegant, very blonde, and proper. They were both proper. Lori Anne said it was the English in them that made them that way. George Golden's dad had emigrated to Dallas, Texas from London when George was just a boy. They made the move along with their best friends, the Knightlys, Brenda's mom and dad.

Mr. Golden owned the only grocery store in Rooster. The long white sign over the entrance to the downtown storefront was trimmed in black and declared in gold letters, "Golden's Grocery & Drug Store." The British-style letters on the sign were also trimmed in black. The store was always the picture of perfection. Every item in place. No dust on the floor or counter. The Goldens were proud people with a sense of style I admired and sometimes imitated when I played alone in my upstairs fort at home.

"Thank you for the compliment," my Dad said and then added, "It was purely by God's grace. This was the most difficult service I have ever done."

Chuck and Willy sat on the floor, backs propped against the wall and paper plates filled with roast, carrots, potatoes and corn resting on their knees. They ate in silence. I sat on the bed with Gib and Lori Anne. Lori Anne was in the middle, between Gib and me, and I could feel the warmth on the outside of my right thigh where her leg touched mine. I stopped straining to hear the adults and concentrated my thoughts on that one section of my leg. Scooping potatoes into my mouth, I glanced sideways at Lori Anne and wondered if she felt my leg like I felt hers—or if she even noticed. If she did she showed no sign of it. She was obviously aching inside for our friend Gib and so was I—and I was mad at myself for letting something like the innocent touch of her leg against mine make me forget what a horrible moment this really was.

What kind of person was I, anyway? If I had been a stronger Christian that day in the graveyard none of this would have ever happened. I had started out concerned about Gib's soul and ended up signing the death warrant for his kid brother. Now, I really felt lousy. I returned my fork to my plate. I suddenly had no appetite. At that moment, not even the tender warmth of Lori Anne's leg could make me feel better.

Willy farted. It was loud, rumbling against the floor. We all stared at him, amazed at his impropriety. Willy looked startled, as if the fart were an Indian that had snuck up on him and taken him by complete surprise. There was total silence as we each looked at the other. Lori Anne rolled her eyes and seemed about to scold the rude boy when Gib lost it. He started out trying to stifle his urge to laugh but the deep convulsions erupted through his tightly closed lips. He made a farting sound himself as the trapped laughter pierced the prison doors of his mouth and then he was holding his stomach, sliding to the floor, sounding like a cross between a braying donkey and an excited blackbird. Tears rolled down his face as he laughed and laughed. Soon we were all on the floor, clutching our stomachs, laughing and squeezing out farts like cannon fire. Even Lori Anne was on her knees, laughing and waving at the foul-smelling fumes that permeated the room.

Mrs. Gillespie threw open the door, "What in the Sam…? Gilbert Gillespie! What for the love of Pete…?" Then she sniffed the air, Declared softly, "I'd be ashamed," and closed the door, assuring Mom and Mrs. Golden that everything was all right.

CHAPTER 8

This Was Heaven

Everything was alright? How could it be? How could anything ever be alright again? I lay in my bed, listening to the steady drumming of the rain against my window, staring into the darkness, pondering that very question. Every few minutes, the lightning would illuminate my room, casting eerie shadows on the wall. I shuddered and closed my eyes, trying to will myself to sleep.

Instead, the images of the day kept marching through my mind. I could see the plain little silver and gray casket. Large sprays of flowers were all around it, with one made of red roses adorning its top. The casket was in front of the pulpit of the Calvary Baptist Church, where the altar normally sat. Behind the pulpit stood my Dad, dressed in his best black suit, white shirt and gray and black tie.

Dad wiped beads of sweat from his furrowed brow and then folded and returned the white hanky to its home in his coat pocket. His speech was slow and deliberate and he seemed to have the slightest hint of a shake in his voice. He read from the book of Job, in the Old Testament: "The Lord giveth and the Lord taketh away: blessed be the name of the Lord."

"Job uttered these immortal words," Dad informed the solemn mourners that crowded our little church building, "on a day when he lost everything that was precious to him—including all of his children." I sat up and listened, but could not take my eyes off of the casket that I knew contained the cold, hard, lifeless body of my best friend's baby brother. Dad continued, "The only way a grieving parent can say words like those in times like these is by faith. I cannot even fathom a faith like this. I know that without the strength of God in one's life, it would be impossible."

The little sanctuary sat in awed silence, except for the occasional sobs of Mrs. Gillespie and others and the mellow, soothing voice of my magnificent father. He was amazing. His voice was salve to the open wounds of our hearts. His words were a colorful and comforting quilt, which he wrapped around our shimmering shoulders as he drew us to the breast of God.

"This is a great loss to us. But we can rest assured that little Jesse, this beautiful fine Christian boy, is in no way suffering now. He is, even as we weep, in the presence of the angels, in the arms of his Savior, in a state of perfect joy and peace."

This was the first funeral I had ever attended. I was sure, though, that no preacher anywhere had ever done a better job of consoling a bereaved family than my Dad was doing right then. He made heaven sound so good, I almost wished I was in the casket instead of poor Jesse. Almost.

Dad rehearsed Job's words again, saying, "The Lord gave us something wonderful in Jesse Gillespie, and the Lord has taken him away. Why? We do not know. Only God knows. So, we are left with two choices. We can become angry and bitter and blame God. Or, we can trust God, even though we don't understand this." Then, Dad paused for a long minute, looked lovingly at Mr. and Mrs. Gillespie, and said, "We love you and hurt with you today. And we pray that God will visit your hearts with His tenderest mercies and crown your home with His matchless grace."

With those words, my Dad bowed his head and prayed like only he could. His words soared upward on eagles' wings, to open the very gates of Heaven itself, and then fluttered like so many angelic feathers upon our hearts.

❧ ❧ ❧

The trip across Lovers' Lane into Rooster Cemetery was another experience altogether. When Dad had concluded his prayer and stepped down beside the casket, Mr. Underwood had moved the roses from atop the casket and opened it to reveal the smiling face and upper torso of little Jesse. I wondered how he could have repaired the horrific dent in the side Jesse's head so neatly.

The dead boy looked contentedly asleep. His cheeks were rosy and his arms were carefully folded across his chest. He wore a new white shirt and his black Sunday overalls. We all filed by the casket one by one. I walked with Mom. Twin streams flowed from my eyes, converging beneath my chin and running in one lazy river down my neck.

When Stu and Maggie Gillespie walked by the casket to see the face of their dead son for the last time, Mrs. Gillespie lost all the composure she had so valiantly maintained for much longer than anyone believed her capable. Her legs buckled and she collapsed onto the corpse that had been her baby boy. She dug at his stiff shoulders to pull him to her heaving bosom. I could feel her anguish in my own chest so heavily I could scarcely breathe.

Dad and Mr. Underwood steadied the casket and the gurney on which it sat while Stu kept Maggie from crumbling all the way to the floor.

The sight of his hysterical mother sent Gib—who had seemed to be mostly in an emotionless trance until that moment—over the edge. He grabbed his Momma's arm and wailed. He cried for Jesse to come back. He said how sorry he was. He begged Jesus, his Mom, my Dad, someone to just give poor Jesse one more chance to live.

With the help of Maggie Gillespie's two older brothers, Matthew and Malcolm, Stu finally was able to separate her from Jesse. Matthew and Stu walked on either side of Mrs. Gillespie, holding her up by her elbows. Her face was buried in Stu's shoulder and I could not make out what she was saying through her muffled sobs. Malcolm had taken Gib by the hand and the two of them followed closely behind. Soon they were out the back doors of the church and disappeared into the big family car provided by Mr. Underwood.

The cemetery was only across the street from the church. Still, people poured into their cars to form a police-escorted processional, courtesy of Deputy Conrad. Rain fell steadily down from the heavens. I stood beside our Cadillac, my hands in my pockets and shoulders hunched against my neck. The rain drenched me thoroughly as I waited for Mom and Rachel to arrive and Mom to unlock the car doors. I squinted against the droplets dripping from my eyebrows, trying to catch a glimpse of my pal, Gib. But he had already disappeared into the family car and I could not see him.

I watched Lori Anne and her parents trot through the rain to their car. Lori turned to smile sadly at me and wave her hand ever so slightly. I smiled and nodded. Even in this painful moment, the sight of earth's most perfect girl soothed my spirit and stirred something inside me. I watched her, enchanted by the gracefulness of her movement and the bouncing coils in her fixed-up hair. Momentarily, I was transported...until some rude intruder blocked my view.

It was Mom. "Reginald! hurry up, son, and get in," she said as she unlocked and opened my door. "You will catch your death of cold." I sat down in the car and immediately a puddle formed around me on the leather seat. The rain felt good to me. It seemed like God was washing the world of the ugliness of poor Jesse's death.

Mom muttered something about ducks and this weather. Then she started the engine, turned on her headlights, and joined the sad, silent string of cars and pickup trucks reverently making their way across Lovers' Lane, through the arched rock gate of Rooster Cemetery, and down the little gravel path that led eventually to the spot where a green tent with the words "Underwood Funeral Home" written in bold white letters across it braced itself against the rain, which was now coming down in buckets.

Underneath the tent four rows of metal chairs were set up, facing the rectangular hole in the earth where poor Jesse's body would soon be buried. The sight of it made me spasm with a chill. With the windshield wipers moving methodically before us, as though they were the twin batons of a skilled conductor, directing the steady hum of the wiper motor to keep pace with rhythmic beat of the rain on the car roof, Mom and Rachel and I watched as the pallbearers, which included three of Maggie's cousins and three men from our church, splashed somberly through the mud, following my Dad, who held his umbrella in one hand and his black bible in the other. The surreal figures moved deliberately, carefully testing each step. With one hand each pallbearer held onto the silver rail that ran down the two long sides of the casket, and with the other he balanced himself.

I wondered what would happen if they dropped poor Jesse.

They didn't. But by the time they reached the casket-lowering contraption that stood over the open grave and beneath the protective covering of the tent and slid the casket across its rollers and on to the green straps, they were a sad sight. Their suits could not have been wetter if they had jumped fully clothed into Rooster Lake. Three of them wore glasses and were desperately fishing for any dry article of clothing to wipe them on. One of Mrs. Gillespie's cousins hurriedly adjusted his thick brown hair, which the rain had knocked cock-eyed on his head. (Gib had once told me a funny story about a second cousin of his who wore a rug where his hair used to be. I guessed this was the fellow.) Their shoes were caked in the mud that also splashed itself halfway up their pants legs. After relieving themselves of their morose burden, the brave men stood dutifully to the side, some of them just outside the tent, the steady downpour adding to their already miserably drenched condition. They trained their eyes on Dad.

My gallant father stood at the head of the casket, in the southeast corner of the tent. He faced the little group of chairs, his puffy hands gripping his bible, and watched as Mr. Underwood and his two associates escorted the family to the metal chairs.

❖ ❖ ❖

Through my window I saw a bolt of lightning that looked like it hit the ground somewhere in the Rooster Cemetery. I was sitting up in my bed now, thinking of poor Jesse out there in that miserable storm, trapped in an air-tight casket, beneath six feet of pure mud. Chill bumps rose on my arms and legs. I pulled the covers around my shoulders and thought more about the unsettling scene beneath Mr. Underwood's graveyard tent.

Mr. Gillespie sat in the middle of the front row of those metal chairs beneath the tent. Gib leaned on one of his broad shoulders and Mrs. Gillespie on the other. Beside Gib sat Eugene, and next to Mrs. Gillespie sat Doreen, her spitting image. They were the driest folks there besides Dad, because Mr. Underwood, always the consummate professional, was prepared for the possibility of foul weather, and provided umbrellas for the bereaving family. Gib's grandparents, the three still living since the death of his Mom's Mom a year ago, occupied the second row. Aunts, uncles, cousins, and assorted other Gillespies and McGradys filled the remaining seats, except for the three on the back row which Mr. Underwood saved for Mom, Rachel and me.

Dad read a passage from 1 Corinthians about how we were not supposed to grieve the same way people without hope grieved. He read about the resurrection, something about corruption putting on incorruption, and mortality taking on immortality. It was all pretty confusing to a ten year old boy who had only dreamed once of being a preacher.

I looked at the people huddled beneath the tent and then around to those for whom there was no room inside it. They were a covey of human quail huddled together in the driving rain. Dad hurried through his Scripture reading, then committed Jesse's young body to the dust from whence it came and his eternal soul to God, and prayed.

It was the shortest prayer I ever heard Dad give.

As soon as he said Amen, people began splashing through the standing water and sinking mud to their cars. Dad and the pallbearers all placed what was left of their boutonnieres on top of Jesse's casket, beside the red rose spray. Then they filed by the first two rows of metal chairs, Dad first, then each of the pallbearers, to shake hands, hug and offer condolences to Mr. and Mrs. Gillespie, Gib, Eugene, Doreen and the three distraught grandparents. I could not make out their words because of the drumming of the rain against the tent and the frequent booms of thunder. Besides, they barely talked above a whisper.

I wondered what Gib was thinking just then. Was he alright?

❧ ❧ ❧

The lightning flashed again, followed immediately by the window-rattling, floor-shaking sonic boom of thunder. In the flash, I saw the ghostly figure of a boy in my window.

I jumped up in my bed and flattened myself against the wall behind me, staring at the window and screaming at the top of my lungs. I didn't usually believe in ghosts, but there was Jesse, back from the dead, staring through my bedroom window. He looked sad and alone, wet and scared.

But he could not have been half as scared as I.

To my dismay, I realized that I wasn't screaming at all. I was trying to, but the cold, clammy hand of fear had me by the throat as it had the night I thought my Dad was dead, so that all I could manage was a hoarse, nearly inaudible whisper.

"Dad!" I shouted so quietly that even I could not hear it. "Dad! Help!"

I couldn't scream. I couldn't move. I was trapped.

Another flash of lightning showed me the boy again, now with his face pressed against the pane. He was rapping on my window.

"Hey! Preach! Let me in."

I stared in wonder at the image in the window, now illuminated by a flashlight beneath his chin. It wasn't my dead little friend, Jesse, rapping at my window.

It was Gib.

* * *

We each held a flashlight in one hand and a pellet gun in the other as we cautiously made our way down the hill that led from my house to town. We walked in the middle of the gravel road; flashlights turned off, so as not to attract attention. I couldn't figure out whether I was more afraid before I knew it was Gib at my window or after he told me why he was there.

"Preach," he had said, "I need your help."

He breathlessly explained that he had been unable to sleep and that he couldn't get the thought out of his head that his brother was out there in that graveyard on such a sorry night as this with no one to look out for him. I argued that Jesse was in heaven and not in the cemetery at all.

"Well, all the Jesse I ever knew was the body that's out there in that graveyard!"

"Gib..."

"'sides, I'm afraid that some of them Joneses or their friends are gonna come and do somethin' to his grave."

"They wouldn't."

"Why not? They hate us! They're ones kilt him, ain't they?"

I had no answer.

"Listen, Preach, if ya don't wanna come, it's ok. But I gotta do this."

When he turned to crawl out my window, I stopped him.

"Wait, Gib. If this is that important to you, I will go. Just give me a minute to get dressed."

"Ok," he seemed relieved, "Bring your gun, too. We might need it."

When we climbed to the top of the rock wall-of-a-fence surrounding Rooster Cemetery, we stopped and sat a-straddle it. We both stared into the pitch black darkness of the city of the dead.

The rain was not a heavy downpour anymore. But it was steady. We were wearing our rain slickers and boots and were in pretty good shape as far as dryness. That is, if I could just keep from peeing my pants from the unsettling idea of walking about in a graveyard in the middle of a night with the death angel still very likely in the near vicinity of Rooster, Texas.

I rested my trusty pellet gun across my lap and whispered, "Gib, we could just keep guard from up here, don't ya think?"

Gib didn't answer. He shined his light onto the ground below, swung his other leg over to the graveyard side of the wall, lowered his rifle until it rested on the ground and against the rock wall. Then he jumped to the ground, gathered his gun, and motioned for me to join him.

I did and we were off, prowlers with pellet guns, plodding across the premises of our original sin, the place where we were warned not to go without our parents or else. The twin beams from our flashlights bounced about in alternately widening ovals and narrowing circles on the ground a few feet ahead of us. We walked carefully, sloshing through the standing water and avoiding any places where grass did not grow. Neither of us wanted to sink shin-deep into a mud hole. We stepped around the big headstones and over the flat grave markers. A few of them I unhappily recognized from our earlier exploits.

All along the way I prayed that we would not get caught and that Jesse and all the rest of the dead would just stay put wherever they were. There was no sound but that of falling rain and the thump-

thump-thumping of my bass drum heart. Neither was there any light but the criss-crossing and bouncing circles on the ground before us and the occasional dull illumination from the lightning that was now somewhere off in the distant northeast.

When we arrived at Jesse's grave, I was surprised. The tent was gone. So was the contraption that had stood over the open grave. There was not yet a headstone of any kind to mark the spot, either. Only a freshly piled mound of mud indicated where the body of my buddy's brother lay. Gib and I stood in total silence for a long time, both of our flashlights shining up and down the length of Jesse's mound. I was aware of this hollow, inexpressible ache somewhere deep inside me. A gnawing pain it was. It made me so sad I wanted to cry and so angry I wanted to yell. But I did neither.

Neither did Gib.

"Well, Preach, there he lies."

"Yeah."

"Sad, ain't it?"

"Yeah."

"Wish it was me."

"Yeah."

Silence.

* * *

We sat back to back, Gib and me. We were straddling a little concrete bench that sat under a weeping willow tree just about fifteen yards from Jesse. I faced the east. Gib, the west.

The rain had stopped. Bullfrogs were calling out in loud, lusty voices to one another or to us or to the dead or to whoever would care to listen.

How long we sat there in uneasy silence is anyone's guess. But the longer we sat, the less nervous I felt. I was beginning to believe that we would not be attacked by anything living or dead—unless it was a bullfrog. And my pellet gun figured to be more than a match for even the biggest croaker in the cemetery.

"Preach?"

"Yeah?"

"What do you reckon Jess is doin' up yonder? In Heaven, I mean."

Good question! Boy, do I wish I had an answer. Gib could sure use one right now. I could just make one up, but he is too smart for that, and it would only make him feel worse. What would Dad say?

"I think he is prob'ly walking along that river they talk about, holdin' hands with Grandma, maybe skipping a rock, if they have 'em there, an' if it's allowed," Gib offered before I could say I didn't know what Jesse was doing just then. Then he added in an unexpectedly happy tone, "When I get there, if I do, I'm gonna run me a trot line. I bet they got rainbow trout big as Volkswagens in that river!"

I had never thought about the fishing in Heaven. But why not? It is Heaven…and what kind of Heaven would it be without a good fishing hole?

I said that the trout fishing in Heaven ought to beat even the spring-fed rivers in the Rocky Mountains of Colorado, which I had read about in my Uncle Roy's copy of *Field and Stream* magazine. And since neither of us had ever caught or even seen a rainbow trout, I said that I would like to go along on that fishing trip.

"Wouldn't think o' doin' it without ya, Preach," said my very best friend in the whole wide world.

It was sometime in the pre-dawn hour when Gib and I stood just outside the rock wall of the graveyard and said goodbye to each other. He had better hurry home, he figured, if he was going to get back in bed before daylight. Otherwise, his Momma might just die, thinking she had lost not one, but two of her boys.

Alone and not really afraid, but plenty worried about finding my Dad standing on the front porch looking for me, I scuttled up the hill, kicking up rocks along the gravel road, keeping my eyes trained on the yellow glow of our porch light, the beacon on the hill. I strained to see if any inside lights were burning.

None were.

I eased up the trunk and into the waiting arms of my old friend, the big Pecan, stealthily moving through the familiar branches until I reached a good place to drop onto the roof. Then, I crawled on hands and knees to my second-story window, slid it open, skinnied through it, put my flashlight, gun and slicker away, undressed, and climbed between my sheets.

I closed my eyes, feeling grand about not giving away our graveyard expedition and even grander about helping my pal through maybe the worst night of his entire life.

I slipped away into Dreamland.

I found myself on the riverbank in Heaven, fishing with Gib, Jesse (who still wore his black Sunday overalls), and, oddly enough, Roy Orrin James. As I looked about I was surprised at how the river in Heaven so resembled the Brazos where Dad, Big Granddad, Uncle Roy, and I always camped and ran trot-lines for channel cat.

I happily hauled in one giant rainbow trout after another until my arms ached from reeling them in. Then, I stripped naked and did a cannonball into the crystal waters.

Soon, everyone was stripping and jumping in with me. We laughed and splashed water at each other and had such fun. Even old Deacon Broadas—who somehow had worked his way into my dream unannounced—was buck naked in the river, slapping the water with his open hands, and laughing like a schoolgirl. There was Lori, too, laughing and squirting me with water from between her shiny brace-bearing teeth.

No one complained or ordered us to get out and put our clothes on.

This was Heaven.

CHAPTER 9

Forty West

When you're traveling west on Interstate Forty, somewhere between Amarillo and Albuquerque, and every mile you drive looks exactly like the one before, and the road is as straight as a sunbeam, and the cruise control is set at seventy, and you are not too distracted by the endless splatter of giant raindrops and the rhythmic slapping of the windshield wipers, you have time to think.

That's what I'm thinking. That, and how the untimely death of my wonderful dad and the sudden memory of a forgotten dream and the warmth of a tender smile have conspired to change my life forever.

* * *

When the phone rang and it was the voice of Big Granddad, I was glad. For a moment. Sitting alone in my over-priced, three-story, two bedroom San Francisco townhome, watching the evening news and doing paperwork from the day's sells, I welcomed the old familiar voice, even if it did always feel like I was getting a call from God himself.

But the news was not good.

"Son," Big Granddad's voice shook, and I had never heard it shake before, and felt a bit shaken by it, even before he continued, "This is Granddad. I have some bad news. Your dad is dead."

Dad is dead. That sentence didn't even make sense. "What do you mean?"

"Your dad died just a few minutes ago. We are here at the Methodist Hospital in Fort Worth. He was having trouble catching his breath, so your mom drove him over here. He had a heart attack. I'm sorry, son. He's gone."

Granddad's tenderness was as unfamiliar to me as his quivering, tear-stained voice. He was usually unflappable. I had seen him bury a number of people, all of whom were important to him, but never did he show much emotion. I made him repeat the news at least three times to be sure I was hearing him right. It was all so surreal. I felt like I was having an out-of-body experience. Like I had gotten hold of some bad drugs. And I didn't even do drugs!

When Mom got on the phone, she was so shaken that I could not understand anything she said. Rachel was no more coherent than she. So, I ended up talking some more to Big Granddad. I learned that my dad had been suffering from serious complications related to his Diabetes. I didn't even know he had Diabetes before that moment. Dad had insisted that there was no sense worrying me with his troubles. He figured I had enough of my own. He died as he lived: protecting his boy.

The numbness I felt lasted for over an hour. It was followed by unrequited rage. I slammed my fist through a wall, knocked a closet door off its track, and said some very hostile things to God. Loudly. So loudly that my neighbor, an old widow named Mrs. Houser, called to see if everything was ok. Of course, it wasn't. And she was sorry for my loss. I was thankful she was sorry. There was little else I could think of at the time to be thankful for.

❧ ❧ ❧

Pulling into Rooster for the first time in eight years brought back this flood of memories. I was amazed at how little the town had changed. It seemed to be its own, self-contained world. Its people lived in a vacuum, oblivious, I think, to the crazy, exponential pace of change that was sweeping the civilized—and sometimes not-so-civilized—world around them. Just a few miles to the east Dallas and Fort Worth had grown together into this huge mass of humanity called the Metroplex. Its population was approaching three million, and growing every day. The city limits sign for Rooster still read, "Population: 735." It was pretty accurate, too, give or take a few souls, depending on which outnumbered the other that year, births or deaths. If anybody new moved into town, somebody old moved farther out, presumably to escape the overcrowding.

The old Gillespie homestead hadn't changed much, except for the addition Stu had built onto the back of the house, enlarging the kitchen and providing a bona fide dining room, and the fresh coat of white paint, and the new front screen door, and the repaired porch. Looked like he had finally gotten around to fixing what he was fixing to fix all those years.

Up the street, around the corner and a couple houses down, the Golden residence was as pristine and well-kept as ever. The Weeping Willow tree in the front yard was bigger, and the house was now painted some earthy tone, but other than that, it was as I left it all those years ago. Mrs Golden still looked good, too, I noticed as she worked on her hands and knees in the garden. I considered stopping to say hello, but thought better of it and headed for downtown.

When I passed the empty lot where young Jesse had died, I noticed that the lot was now well grassed, manicured, and no longer contained the old Buick. Instead there was a nice, new playground set and a sign that read, "Jesse Gillespie Park." I later learned that Mr. Golden and Doc White had bought it and cleaned it up and donated it to the citizens of Rooster, hoping, I suppose, that the laughter of today's children might ease the pain of yesterday's.

Driving through downtown I noted that most of the buildings were boarded up. Only Rooster Hardware, Golden's Grocery, Palo Pinto Feed, and Ben Mallory's Barber Shop were still doing business in the buildings that lined two city blocks on Main Street. A couple of blocks from there Ma Baker still operated the Rooster Café.

Walking around on the black top parking lot of the Calvary Baptist Church was a dose of harsh reality. Maybe not much had changed in Rooster, but this place sure had. Gone was the little white church building with its over-sized steeple. Gone was the pea gravel parking lot. Gone was the old maple-colored pulpit. The hard pews and little altar where I gave my heart to Jesus were gone too. All that was left were the stained-glass windows, which had been carefully preserved from the old building and used in the new dark-red brick building, which now proudly occupied the corner lot and rudely obscured so many of my mental images of yesterday. I had known that the church folk had finally fulfilled Dad's dream and built the new building nearly five years before. I just didn't know how it would make me feel.

I closed my eyes and conjured up images of my dad preaching and praying and Gib and me laughing and playing on those premises. Precious memories. How they lingered.

Mom burst into tears when I walked through the Mahogany front door of my childhood home. I hugged her for a long time, telling her how sorry I was. I was sorry Dad was gone. I was sorry I was not there. I was sorry I did not know how sick he was. I was sorry I hadn't called him more often.

And she was sorry, too. She was sorry I didn't get to say goodbye to Dad. She was sorry I had to be out there in California all alone when I got the bad news. She was sorry that I had to make the long journey home all by myself.

But she was also glad. She was glad we were together again, her and Rachel and me. Of course, she was glad that Rachel's husband, Bryce, and her two kids, Danny (named for Dad) and BJ (for Bryce Jr.) were there too.

"Reginald, you look so tired. Why don't you go take a nice long bath and rest awhile before we go to the funeral home to see your father?"

"Thanks, Mom. I am a little weary."

"Reg?" an excited and familiar voice squealed. It was Rachel, coming through the swinging door from the dining room. "Reg! I am so glad you are here."

I hugged Rachel and we both cried.

"The boys are so big!" I said.

"Danny is ten and BJ is eight and a half already. You haven't seen them in…how long?"

I couldn't remember if it was five or six years since she and Bryce had come to visit me in California.

"Oh well," she sighed. "You're here now. That is what counts. Gosh, it is so good to see you."

We hugged again. She cried some more.

"Dad looks really good," Rachel told me. "Mr. Underwood did a wonderful job. He really loved Dad. You knew he joined our church last year?"

"No. Really?"

"Yeah. He said Dad had made a Baptist of him through his funeral sermons over the years."

Dad had told Mr. Underwood that he didn't have to be a Baptist to go to Heaven, of course, but as long as he was going anyway, he might as well travel first class. Then Dad laughed, and so did the good doctor.

Rachel and I laughed. Dad had a way of making his way seem like the only way, sometimes without even trying. I would soon learn that Dad's church had become the largest in town. His twenty years in Rooster had changed a lot of folks' way of thinking about things religious in nature. Doc White speculated that Dad had become the town's most influential preacher since Roy Orrin James himself. Doc had joined Dad's church too.

So had the Goldens.

❧ ❧ ❧

I slept an hour in my old upstairs bedroom. My feet hung off the end of the twin bed, but my rest was peaceful and mostly dreamless. Then I woke up, took a shower and put on dress slacks and a button-down shirt.

When I came downstairs, I stopped breathing and stared.

There was Lori Anne Golden. Not the Lori I had last seen when we were seniors in college, and she was crying and telling me she loved somebody else. Not the Lori whose hand I held for the first time at the Dairy Queen in Ranger when we were in the seventh grade. Not the Lori whose lips I first kissed on the bus ride home from a football game against Gordon one frosty Friday night when we were high school freshmen. Not the beautiful, five foot eight Lori with the freshly-permed auburn hair, the haunting eyes, and the hourglass figure, whose picture I kept in my top dresser drawer back home in San Francisco. Not that Lori.

No. It was the Lori Anne I saw that first day of school my fifth grade year. Her hair was longer and her eyes were blue. But it was her—ten years old again and standing right before me. She was laughing and talking with my nephew Danny and I recognized in him the awe-struck, tongue-tied nervousness I had felt every time I was in her presence.

"Hi Reg."

I turned to face her. She wore her hair short and stylish. She was dressed in a slinky white blouse and black dress pants. Her perfectly symmetrical nose was slightly flared. Her complexion was perfect, as always. And she had a sad smile painted on her rich, full, enchanting lips.

I stared at her and then looked at her spitting image.

"I see you have met Kelsi."

"Well, uh, no. I mean, I just saw her and thought…My God, she is a carbon copy of you, Lori!"

Lori called Kelsi over. "Kel, this is Reg. He is an old friend. Reg, this is Kelsi, my daughter."

Do I look as dumbfounded as I feel?

The perfect little angel studied me for a long time. "I know you. You used to be Mommy's boyfriend. She has lots of pictures of you in…"

"Ok," Lori interrupted, "Go visit with Danny and BJ."

"Ok, Mommy." She turned to walk away, then paused, turned to me, flipping her long hair over her shoulder, flashing a sweet smile, and sporting a somewhat mischievous glint in her deep blue eyes, and said, "It was really nice to meet you, Mr. Reynolds."

"Yeah," I stammered, still tongue-tied after all these years, "Nice to meet you too, Kelsi."

"Lori," I said, "I had no idea."

"Yes, I know. Your mother told me that you asked not to be told anything about me."

She sounded hurt.

"How old is she?"

"She's ten. She will be in sixth grade next year."

"The same age you were when I met you," I said wistfully.

"I know, Reg. That was a long time ago."

"Yeah," I sighed, painfully aware of the smattering of gray hairs on my head.

"You look great, Reg."

"You do too," I answered honestly.

"I am so sorry about your dad. I know how much he means to you."

"Yeah. Thanks."

"He was one of the best men I have ever known. I loved him too, you know."

"Yeah."

❧ ❧ ❧

Looking in my rearview mirror I see the lights of the sprawling city receding from view.

Albuquerque? How in the world did I pass through Albuquerque without noticing it? I'll be dadgum!

I notice that my wipers are scraping against a now-dry windshield. I laugh at myself and pull off at the Love's truck stop to gas up, stretch my legs, and use the restroom.

She still does it to me. Think of her and I can't think of anything else. Oh well, maybe I will notice when I go through Flagstaff.

Maybe.

❧ ❧ ❧

When Lori and Gib and I graduated high school we each had somewhere different we wanted to go. I was going to seminary in Fort Worth to prepare myself to be a preacher, which pleased my dad immensely. Gib had joined the Marines months before graduation and was headed for basic training at Camp Pendleton. Lori was pursuing her dream of being a lawyer. In Houston.

We all promised to stay in touch. We would call each other every week. We swore that we would be best friends forever. I promised that some day when I had my act together I would propose to Lori. She promised that when that glad day came she would happily say yes.

We lied.

Gib was soon shipped to Europe. I was immersed in the deep mysteries and hard questions of theology. And Lori…fell in love.

He was a senior when she was a freshman. He was dashing and handsome and charismatic and charming and a budding businessman. But most of all, he was there. She saw him every day. They talked. They laughed. They kissed.

I did not know about Spence Thurman until Lori and I were both seniors in college. I knew that Lori seemed different. I knew that she was distant. I knew that she always seemed anxious to get out of Rooster and back to Houston. But Christmas Break 1983, she finally told me. She didn't love me. She loved him. They were getting married. He had just proposed. She was so sorry, but she knew I would find the right one for me. I started to tell her I had already found the only one for me—way back in fifth grade. But I didn't. Instead, I walked away without a word.

My devastation was complete and radical. I never returned to finish my senior year and get my theology degree. My dad became angry and frustrated with me as he saw me sinking into a troubling pit of depression. That summer he bought me a plane ticket to visit David, his brother in California, the one who owned Reynolds Classic Imports in downtown San Francisco. He figured I could go out there, sell cars over the summer, clear my mind, heal my wounds, and come home.

I stayed.

We were huddled together in the little visitation room of Underwood's Funeral Home. The casket was open and I was standing beside Dad, holding his cold, hard hand and telling him everything I hadn't said in eight years. That I loved him. That I was proud of him. That he was my hero and everything I wanted to be.

Mom and Rachel were visiting with the folks who streamed in to pay their respects and tell us all how wonderful Dad was and what he meant to the community in general and them in particular. Some hugged me and cried on my shoulder. Others seemed uncomfortable and uncertain what to say to me. A few of the newcomers didn't know who I was at all.

The strong hand that gripped my shoulder had a familiar feel to it and the voice was an instant antisthetic to the raging pain I felt all over.

"Hey, Preach!"

"Gib!"

I turned, extending my hand to shake his. He knocked it aside, wrapping me in a terrific bear hug. He was about six foot three now, two inches taller than I, and still as skinny as a rail. He wore his hair high and tight, just like the old days. His cheeks still sported splotchy red patches and were smothered in freckles. And he held in his hand the white beaver-skin cowboy hat that I was sure belonged to Deputy Conrad.

"Nope! It's mine."

Gib pulled at his badge with his thumb. It read, "Palo Pinto County Sheriff."

"Sheriff? Really?"

"Yup! Ol' Joe Conrad got hisself 'lected back in '86. I hired on as a deputy a coupla years ago, an' when Joe was kilt in the line o' duty, I was appointed sheriff. The 'lectorate made it official just this May."

Gib went on to explain how Joe Conrad had made what he thought was a routine traffic stop out on Interstate Twenty and ended up getting shot by two guys who were drug runners.

"Dadgum!" I said.

Then Gib motioned a muscular fellow over to him. The man was short of six feet but had huge arms and a thick neck and a full mustache and looked a lot like the Jones boy who had killed young Jesse all those years ago. He was wearing a deputy's badge and holding a cowboy hat in his big hands.

Gib clapped him on the shoulder.

"Remember this ugly mug, Reg?"

"I-I'm not sure."

Gib pointed to the scar on his cheekbone. I looked at the muscular deputy more closely. There was no crusted snot under his nose and he didn't smell bad, but there was no mistaking him.

"Patrick? Patrick Jones?!"

"Yup. He's my best deputy, Preach."

"Dadgum."

"Reg," Patrick said politely and sheepishly, "Real sorry about your dad. He's a goodun."

"Thanks."

I must have looked like I had seen a ghost from the Rooster Cemetery or something.

"Preach, folks change," Gib said. "Turns out ol' Pat ain't no damn retard a tall." Gib shot a glance over each shoulder and reddened at the language slippage at such a place. Then, he continued, "He's just quiet and shy and has a little trouble reading, but hell in a fight, as you know, and good as gold."

"Buried my ol' dad four years ago, Reg," said Patrick. "He had come to really admire yore daddy. Seems yore dad helped 'im get sober and find God. He also helped a lot in the healing between the Gillespies and us."

"What about…"

"Jake?" Patrick anticipated my question.

"Yeah."

"He's in the state penitentiary. You know they tried him as an adult an' he spent those 'leven an' a half years in the pen for killin' little Jess. Well, he got out an' din't change his ways a tall. He got into trouble brawlin' and druggin' down in San Antone. I ain't heard from 'im in five years or more."

"Dadgum," I said more to myself than them.

"Preach, I am so sorry about Ol' Preacher," said Gib. His voice quivered and his eyes glistened as he looked over my shoulder at Dad.

"Thanks, Gib. Gosh, it is so good to see you, old friend."

"You know, me 'n Pat here is both deacons in yore daddy's church now."

I didn't know. Couldn't believe it.

* * *

Other visitors of note that night included Wee Willy Hernandez, who was still wearing his blue work uniform. (Gib said he looked like a half-eaten burrito, and Willy laughed.) Willy's dad had been Rooster's only mechanic, running Rooster Automotive Repair, which Doc White opened way back in the early sixties, mainly because he got weary of having to drive to Ranger or Palo Pinto to get his car worked on. Mr. Hernandez talked Doc into hiring his son when Willy was still a senior in high school to help with the bustling little business. In the mid-eighties, Doc White, in a magnanimous gesture of generosity, gave the business to his loyal employee, who immediately developed cancer and died six months later. Willy inherited the shop and still runs it.

Phil Farmer, who worked for the same trucking company his dad still drove for, was not fat anymore. He had undergone some sort of surgery—Gib said he had his tubes tied, and then laughed hard at his own joke—and lost over two hundred pounds. His skin was loose and saggy, but he looked and felt great. Chuck Illich flew in from New Jersey, where he served as a back-up forward for the NBA team there, to pay his respects to Dad. He was now seven feet tall.

Stu and Maggie Gillespie looked the same, but older and sadder. The Goldens looked the same, and not a bit older. Doc White looked like death warmed over, and Mr. Underwood was inching closer every day to becoming his own customer, as Diabetes ate away at him.

I looked around the room and thought how much Dad would love to get up and visit with all of these fine folks one last time.

❧ ❧ ❧

The funeral was the next afternoon, a Friday. The service was a blur, as my emotions ebbed and flowed and my tears ran their usual course down my chafing cheeks. Sam Sneed, now in his seventies and using a cane to get around, spoke with great emotion as he eulogized his old friend. Big Granddad said his part. He was never eloquent, but always sincere. He cried when he said the final prayer.

The church was packed way beyond capacity, with people standing in the foyer and spilling out onto the front porch. All of Rooster, it seemed to me, had come to say goodbye to the preacher they had once maligned as bringing demon seed to town.

The pallbearers were Stu, Gib, Doc White, Bryce, Patrick Jones, and Roy. (Roy looked great, except for his bald head and slightly rounded belly. He was now the pastor of Big Granddad's old church back in Mineral Wells, Big Granddad having retired five years before.)They had thought about carrying Dad across the street and to the grave rather than placing him in a car, a kind of special honor for the well-loved preacher. But Mom said that Dad was a Cadillac man and would insist, if he could, on riding in style. I figured she was thinking more of Doc White and Stu, who were both pretty feeble, than Dad. I think they figured as much too, and appreciated it.

So Dad rode, chauffeured by Mr. Underwood himself, while the rest of us walked. Malcolm Gillespie, whom I had not seen since Jesse's funeral, wore a kilt and played Amazing Grace on the bagpipes as he led the mourners through the old cemetery. It was very moving, and I barely noticed the sweltering heat.

I did, however, notice the elegant, entrancing beauty of Lori Anne Golden as she walked sadly behind her father and mother, holding Kelsi's hand.

* * *

It was nearly midnight. I was sitting on the same bench Gib and I had occupied that rainy night of Jesse's funeral, staring at the mound that represented my Dad. I needed some time alone with him. I needed to tell him that I had never forgotten the promise I made when I was fifteen, when I finally eased the burden of that dream and told God I would be a preacher. I needed to tell him that I thought about him every day and that whenever I found myself confused or in trouble, I always asked, "What would Dad do?" I didn't always do what he would do. I knew that. But I thought about it. And that counts for something, doesn't it?

In the moonlight, I watched the dark, shadowy figure of Gib walking slowly toward me.

"Preach? Want some company?"

"Sure."

"You were always there for me, Preach. I wanna be here for you."

"Thanks."

"Gets confusin', don't it?"

"What does?"

"All this dyin'…and even the livin'."

"Yeah."

"Yore daddy never gave up on the dream of you bein' a preacher, you know."

"I know."

"Neither has the rest of us."

"What do you mean?"

"Well, we all remember what a fine preacher you was, even as a boy. You were even better'n him," he pointed to Dad's mound. "And he was the best."

I had all but forgotten the preaching I had done while in high school and college. I was preaching revival meetings and youth gatherings all around Palo Pinto county and even in some Metroplex churches. People always said I had a gift. I felt more like a freak, being the only teenage boy I knew who was actually preaching real sermons in bona fide churches.

"Preach," Gib was sounding thoughtful and serious, "You cain't just throw it away or pretend it ain't real. God has given you a gift. You gotta use it."

I said nothing.

"Me an' the rest of the deacons have met and we all agree. We want you to come take over for yore daddy. We want you to come be our preacher."

I stared at Gib in stunned silence.

"Ol' Sam Sneed says he is willin' to fill the pulpit until we find someone permanent. He is too old an' tired to travel anymore. So, this would be a good thing for him and us, we figure. We don't intend to look nowheres else until you say if you will do it or not."

I started to answer that I could not do it, would not do it.

"Hell, Preach—'scuse the language—anybody can sell a bunch of dam…uh, dadgum cars to those fruits and nuts in Californy. We need us a preacher an' you need to be preachin'."

I still could not think of anything to say.

"Just think 'bout it. No hurry. If you'll just say you will think about it, we'll wait."

"I just don't think…I don't know."

"Ok, Preach. We'll wait."

I got up to leave and thanked Gib for being my friend and believing in me. He said it was no trouble and that I should try believing in myself a little. Then he said, "Go see Lori 'fore you leave, Preach. Talk to her."

"What for?"

❧ ❧ ❧

Flagstaff, Arizona! Already? Dadgum!

❧ ❧ ❧

Gib dragged me back down to the bench and told me all about Lori Anne's sad life. Spence Thurman was no prize. He had a fierce temper and frequently beat Lori up. He was especially mean when his business was going badly or when he was drinking, both of which were way too often. When he hit little Kelsi across the cheek a year and a half ago, Lori left him and moved back to Rooster. Spence showed up at the Golden residence a few days later, brandishing and firing off a handgun, and spewing threats. Gib answered the disturbance call, disarmed Spence, beat him senseless, and threw him in jail. A deal was cut. No charges would be filed as long as he gave Lori a divorce and full custody of Kelsi. He signed the agreement before Judge Thomas in the Palo Pinto County Courthouse. Then he got into his pickup and headed back to Houston. Somewhere along the way, he bought a bottle of Jack Daniels and drank it all. Before he got to Houston, just outside of Sugar Land, Spence apparently passed out at the wheel and left the road with his cruise control set at about seventy-five, plowed through a barbed wire fence, and broad-sided a two ton bull. Spence was thrown through the windshield and was found dead with the pulverized bull and the mutilated pickup on top of him.

"Good riddance, too," said Gib. Then, "Preach, she never quit loving you."

"Then why did she do it, Gib?"

"She was scared o' you bein' a preacher an' all. She thought you were too good for her and that she would just slow you down."

"Too good? Too good?" I yelled it, jumping to my feet. "She's the best person I know. How could someone like me be too good for her?"

"Go see her. Tell her that."

Gib, who was married to Lori's best friend, Monica Mallory, I knew loved and admired Lori Anne as much as I ever had. I often feared that I would have to contend with him for Lori's affection some day. But he was my friend…and she was my girl. And that was the way of it.

"Preach, she has been real nervous 'bout seein' you. Don't judge her too harsh. She's been through a lot."

"I know."

"I best get home afore Monica calls the sheriff," Gib joked. We hugged. I cried. He left.

I decided not to go see Lori. Instead, I spent the next two days with Mom and Rachel and her boys. I didn't venture out of the house at all during the day, but stole quietly to the old cemetery each night to cry some more and talk to Dad. I also visited with young Jesse and Roy Orrin James. Through the years of my youth I had often gone to this solitary place to think and talk to those who could only listen and never answer.

Then I packed my shiny new Jaguar and headed west. I would leave again…without a word.

I was passing through Palo Pinto when I heard the siren and saw the red lights flashing.

Dadgum it!

I pulled over and fumbled for my wallet, cursing the poor timing of it all. There was a rapping on my window and I rolled it down and handed my driver's license to…her.

"Reginald Reynolds, is this the only way you know to handle me? Just drive away?"

I looked at Lori standing beside my car in her blue jeans and spaghetti string top and all of those old feelings stirred themselves from deep inside me.

"You are going to talk to me this time, Reg."

I unlocked the car doors and asked her to get in. She did.

"I am sorry. I'm sorry I hurt you, Reg. But you hurt me too. I wanted you to fight for me. I wanted you to stand up to me and tell me that I was yours and no one else's. You just walked away."

"You said you loved him."

"I loved you. I always have."

I looked down at my shoes and said nothing. I could feel her studying me. I could sense her tears, her pain. I said nothing.

"Well," she said, "I came to say I'm sorry and to give you this."

She handed me a leather-bound journal. It had my name engraved on it.

"Goodbye, Reg."

Lori got out of the car, shut the door, and walked away. I opened the journal and found a note on the first page. This is what it read:

Dearest Reg,

I wanted to say that I am sorry. I am sorry I lied about my love for you. I am sorry about your father's death. I am sorry for the pain you have felt.

You have always had a way with words. You are a great speaker and a good writer. You have been through so much in your life, I just thought it might help you to write it down. I hope you will write about the good things and the good times, and not just the bad.

I still believe in you. I still believe in happy endings. I hope that, whatever you write in this journal, it will have a happy ending. You deserve it.

All My Love,

Lori

❧ ❧ ❧

I watched in my rearview mirror as Gib turned off his lights and made a u-turn to take Lori home to Rooster. Then, I was out of my silver Jaguar, into the middle of the road, chasing them and waving my arms and yelling as loud as I could.

Gib was a quarter-mile down the road when he slammed on the brakes. He backed up to the place where I stood on the yellow stripe, the occasional car swerving to the shoulder of the road and passing curiously by. One made a gesture and hollered that I was a blankety-blank fool, then looked at Gib in his sheriff's uniform and returned hastily to his own business.

I opened Lori's door and pulled her from the car.

"Tell me this, Lori Anne Golden," I said between breathless gasps, "In this happy ending of yours, does the boy get the girl?"

"Only if he wants her."

She smiled. I threw my arms around her waist, drew her tightly to me, and kissed her. I kissed her for the love I felt in my heart. I kissed her for the joy she had brought to my life. I kissed her for all the time we had lost, and for all the time we had left.

Gib had turned his siren and lights on and was waving cars around us. We paid him no attention at all.

Epilogue: Better Late Than Never

It's August in the Mojave desert. I am in the McDonald's in Barstow, California, watching a group of happy kids huddled around the egg they are frying on the sidewalk. My U-Haul truck is loaded down and pointed east. I am thinking of the future. Lori and I will be married in two weeks. Gib will stand with me, and Monica with her. Roy will do the honors and lead us through our vows. We will go on a Caribbean cruise for our honeymoon. I will adopt Kelsi and get to work right away on adding a Gilbert Daniel Reynolds to our happy family. The deacons have already put my name on the new church sign, Mom says. Lori is busy fixing up the house we are buying, just one block from where Gib and Monica and their boys, Jesse and Reg, live.

I am thinking, dear journal, of the future while I tell you all about the past. There was pain. There was loss. There were mistakes and misunderstandings.

But that was then.

This is now.

About the Author

L.A. Holly is a secondary school teacher. He lives in Grand Prairie, Texas with his wife, three daughters, and a Schnauzer named Scotty.

0-595-22491-1

Printed in the United States
45734LVS00004B/231

9 780595 224913